George Reynolds

The Myth of the Manuscript Found

The Absurdities of the Spaulding Story

George Reynolds

The Myth of the Manuscript Found
The Absurdities of the Spaulding Story

ISBN/EAN: 9783337183158

Printed in Europe, USA, Canada, Australia, Japan

Cover: Foto ©Andreas Hilbeck / pixelio.de

More available books at **www.hansebooks.com**

THE MYTH OF THE

"MANUSCRIPT FOUND."

OR THE

ABSURDITIES OF THE

"SPAULDING STORY."

•—■—•

ELEVENTH BOOK OF

THE ⸭ FAITH-PROMOTING ⸭ SERIES.

——— •◆• ——

BY ELDER GEORGE REYNOLDS.

——— •◆• ———

Designed for the Instruction and Encouragement
of young Latter-day Saints.

◆ ◆ •

JUVENILE INSTRUCTOR OFFICE,

Salt Lake City, Utah.

1883.

PREFACE.

THE previous numbers of the FAITH-PROMOTING SERIES have consisted largely of the personal narratives of men of God living in these days, in which it has been shown how the Lord preserves, protects, guides, inspires and directs His servants in this dispensation, and reveals His word and will to them after the manner and by like methods to those by which He manifested himself to the righteous in the ages of the past, demonstrating His unchangeableness and the validity of our claim that we are His acknowledged people. With feelings of intense joy, deep devotion and profound gratitude to Him, the previous numbers of this Series have been read by thousands of Latter day Saints. This little volume takes a somewhat new departure. It treats of a book—a divine record, the true story of its discovery and translation, and of the falsehoods that have been invented, nourished and sown broadcast throughout Christendom to blind men's eyes to its real import. For the Book of Mormon being true then Joseph Smith is a prophet of God and "Mormonism" is the everlasting gospel of our Lord Jesus Christ; but if it were a forgery, as our enemies assert, then would all our hopes be vain and our faith worthless.

The so-called "Spaulding story" has been for many years past the last refuge of those who have undertaken to prove that the Book of Mormon is not what it claims to be. All other hypothesis have long since been committed to limbo as too silly, too outrageous or too inconsistent even for a gullable anti-"Mormon" public. In this short treatise we have endeavored to prove the utter untenability of this theory. We have shown that the upholders of this myth are not only at variance with each other, but that all their assertions are inconsistent with the well-known facts associated with its discovery; and when we proceed further to examine the internal evidence of the book we very soon discover that the conglomeration of conjectures, guesses, suppositions, etc., of which this "Spaulding story" is formed is "as unstable as water" and utterly unworthy of belief.

The individual testimonies of the three witnesses gathered from many authentic sources are an important feature of this little work. With true Latter-day Saints they must inevitably be a source of joy and consolation, and none who are honest, be they "Mormons" or not, can rise from the perusal of their simple statements without realizing a marked effect therefrom. They bear the impress of truth, sincerity and genuineness in every paragraph.

In conclusion we dedicate these pages to God, to His people and to all who love the right, trusting that their mission will not be without effect in the spread of His righteousness and the dissemination of His truth.

G. R.

Salt Lake City,
August 7th, 1883.

CONTENTS.

THE MYTH OF THE MANU-
SCRIPT FOUND.

CHAPTER I.

THE HISTORY OF THE MANUSCRIPT.

TIME and again, at recurring intervals of unequal length, the Church of Jesus Christ of Latter-day Saints is assailed with a rehash of the notorious "Spaulding story," which from frequent repetition has become as familiar in the mouths of many of the Saints as household words. True, the story in its details is not always identical, it is altered, re-arranged, or "cooked" to suit the necessities of the story teller, but in its essential particulars it remains the same. Its burden is that a certain "reverend" gentleman of Conneaut, Ohio, named Solomon Spaulding, in the early part of the present century, wrote a historical romance which he entitled the "Manuscript Found," that in some unexplained and unexplainable way, but generally imagined to have been through Sidney Rigdon, the youthful Joseph Smith obtained access to this manuscript and from its scanty pages elaborated the Book of Mormon, which he afterwards palmed upon the world as a divine revelation.

This is the substance of the "Spaulding story." It is a frantic effort to prove the Book of Mormon a forgery and a fraud, for it is very evident that if the Book of Mormon is not of God then the whole superstructure of "Mormonism is of nec

1

essity a gross imposture, the cruelest of religious deception that
for many centuries has misled humanity. All other theories
advanced to prove this record false having long since failed,
the "Spaulding story" is the last and only resort of those who
oppose the divine mission of Joseph Smith, and though many
a time refuted and proved an impossiblity, yet, it is that
or nothing; and the malignant hatred of the wicked not permitting the Book of Mormon to stand on its own intrinsic
merits, or be judged by its own internal evidences, this story
has to be again and again revamped as the last hope of a hope-
less cause which perceives in the triumph of "Mormonism"
the seal of its own destruction. To consider this story, its
origination and history, its claims on the credulity of mankind,
and the weight of evidence for and against it, will be topic of
the following pages.

Attention has been drawn and interest created anew in Mr.
Spaulding and his unpublished romance by the appearance in
the public prints of articles and affidavits by members of his
family, in which the story of the "Manuscript Found" is
given, and efforts made to connect it with the Book of Mormon. Among the most important of these papers is an affidavit of Mrs. McKinstry the daughter of Mr. Spaulding, which
gives a history of the manuscript from the time it was written
until it passed out of the hands of the family. We will first
draw attention to the various points made by Mrs. McKinstry
from her actual knowledge, leaving out those reflections, suppositions and vain imaginings in which she indulges when she
wanders from the path of her actual knowledge; but lest it
should be asserted that we have not fairly represented her
statements, we insert the affidavit in full as an appendix to this
little volume.

According to Mrs. McKinstry's affidavit she resided with
her father, Mr. Solomon Spaulding, at Conneaut, Ohio, in 1812,
she then being a child in her sixth year.

About this time her father was very much interested in the
antiquities of this continent, and wrote a romance on the subject, which he called the "Manuscript Found," in which she
believes the names of Mormon, Moroni, Nephi and Lamanite
appear.

This was not the only work of Mr. Spaulding, he was a man of literary tastes and wrote a number of tales. etc., which he was in the habit of reading to his family, to his little daughter, now Mrs. McKinstry, among the rest.

From Conneaut the family removed to Pittsburg, Pennsylvania, where they had a friend named Patterson, a bookseller. To this gentleman, her mother states, the ''Manuscript Found'' was loaned and by him read, admired and returned to the author.

The stay of the family in Pittsburg was very brief, for they shortly removed to Amity, Pennsylvania, where Mr. Spaulding died in 1816. Immediately afterwards she and her widowed mother paid a visit to the latter's brother Mr. William H. Sabine, at Onondaga Valley, Onondaga Co., New York. A trunk containing all the writings of the deceased clergyman was taken with them and in this trunk was the "Manuscript Found." While here Mrs. McKinstry saw and handled the manuscript and describes it as closely written and about an inch thick.

Afterwards her mother went to reside with her father (Mrs. McKinstry's grandfather) at Pomfret, Connecticut, but she did not take the trunk of manuscript with her. In 1820 she again married and became the wife of a Mr. Davison, of Hardwicks, near Coopertown, New York. After her marriage she sent for her things left at her brother's, among the rest the old trunk of manuscript. These reached her in safety.

In 1828, Mrs. McKinstry was herself married, and resided in Monson, Hampton Co., Mass. Very soon after her marriage her mother joined her there, and was with her most of the time until the latter's death, which took place in 1844.

Mrs. Davison when she went to reside with her daughter left the trunk of manuscript at Hardwicks, in care of Mr. Jerome Clark.

In 1834, one Hurlburt visited her. He bore a letter from her brother, Mr. Sabine, and requested the loan of the "Manuscript Found." She reluctantly gave him a letter addressed to Mr. Clark, at Hardwicks, to deliver him the manuscript; Hurlburt having made repeated promises to return it.

The family afterwards heard that Hurlburt received the manuscript from Mr. Clark, but from that time the Spaulding family never again had it in their possession, though they repeatedly wrote to Hurlburt about the matter.

In the above we have the history of the notorious manuscript from the time it was written until it fell into the hands of D. P. Hurlburt, who was the first man who endeavored to connect it with the Book of Mormon.   Its history may be thus summed up:

Written in 1812 at Conneaut, Ohio.

Taken to Pittsburg shortly after. (1814.)

Thence to Amity, where it was in the possession of its author when he died in 1816.

In 1816 taken to Onondaga Valley, New York.

In 1820 removed to Hardwicks, New York, where it remained until 1834, when it was handed to Hurlburt.

Here we have an unbroken history of its wanderings until years after the Book of Mormon was published.

How then is it presumed that Joseph Smith obtained possession of it? This is an unanswered question. Was Joseph in any of those places at the time the manuscript was there? No, there is not the least proof that he ever was, all the testimony and evidence is directly to the contrary. Was Sidney Rigdon ever in these places?   Not at the same time as the "Manuscript Found," as we shall presently show.

The Prophet Joseph Smith was born in Vermont, December 23rd, 1805, and was consequently in his sixth year when the romance was written. He was only fifteen when it was taken to Hardwicks.   It would be preposterous to imagine that before that age any such labor as the changing of the "Manuscript Found" into the Book of Mormon could be accomplished by one so young, so inexperienced, and withal so ignorant.   For all admit, both friend and foe, that his education at that time was very limited.   In 1820, he received his first vision, and began his prophetic work, being then a resident of Manchester, New York.

In 1823 he still resided with his parents at Manchester, and it was in that year that he first began bearing testimony with regard to the coming forth of what we now call the Book of Mormon, and that he had seen the plates from which it would be translated. Manchester is from 80 to 100 miles from Hardwicks in a direct line, and in the last-named place the "Manuscript" still remained hidden in an old trunk in a garret, no one knowing or expecting that recourse would be had to it for such a base purpose.

Joseph continued to live with his father's family. It is not until 1825, that we have any account of his leaving home for any length of time; until then, when not employed on the farm, he hired out by the day to his neighbors in Manchester and vicinity.

CHAPTER II.

THE ORIGINATOR OF THE SPAULDING STORY.

DOCTOR PHILASTUS HURLBURT was the originator or inventor of the "Spaulding Story."

He was not a doctor by profession, but his mother gave him that name because he was the seventh son, a very common custom in some parts at the time he was born.

Those who adopt his fabrication with regard to the authorship of the Book of Mormon would have people believe that he really was a doctor. It gives an air of respectability to their tale, and tends to make the public think that he must have been a man of good education, though he really was not.

We will now give some statements with regard to his life, and the causes that led to the invention of the desperate lie, regarding the Book of Mormon, which has tended to deceive so many people. These statements are, for the most part, abridged from the writings of one who was intimately acquainted with him.

Hurlburt embraced the gospel in 1832. Previous to this he had been a local preacher in the Methodist church, but had been expelled therefrom for unchaste conduct. Soon after his baptism he went to Kirtland, where he was ordained an Elder. In the Spring of 1833, he labored and preached in Pennsylvania. Here his self-importance, pride and other undesirable traits of conduct soon shook the confidence of the members of the Church in him as a man of God; and before long his unvirtuous habits were so plainly manifested that he was cast off from the Church, and his license taken from him by the conference.

Some may here ask, "How is it that men who leave the Church of Christ and come out in opposition to its truths are so often proven to have previously been men of immoral lives?" The answer is plain and simple: pure, honest, virtuous men do not apostatize and turn against the principles of the gospel. They remain faithful. But men who have been wicked, and who do not sincerely repent when they enter the Church, though they may profess to do so, are very apt to turn aside and fight against God's cause. It is for this reason that so many men of Hurlburt's stamp have, unfortunately for them, been proven to have led very wicked lives before their baptism. Had their repentance been sincere, their after lives would have been different.

Hurlburt went to Kirtland, the seat of the government of the Church, and appealed to the general conference. His case was there reconsidered, and because of his confession and apparent repentance his license was restored to him.

On his way back to Pennsylvania he stopped in Ohio. There he attempted to seduce a young lady, but his design was frustrated. For this crime he was expelled from the Church. Finding he would be tolerated by the Saints no longer, he determined to be revenged by injuring them to the utmost extent of his power. He went to Springfield, Pennsylvania, and commenced to preach against "Mormonism." Here he was received with open arms by those who were vainly endeavoring to stay the progress of God's work in that region, and churches, chapels and meeting houses were crowded to hear him.

He was now dubbed the Rev. Mr. Hurlburt, and was petted and patronized by priest and people; but for all that he did very little in staying the progress of the truth. As an anti-"Mormon" lecturer he was a failure.

During his stay in Pennsylvania, Hurlburt formed many acquaintances, and mingled with all sorts of people. While in a small settlement called Jackson, he became familiar with a family of the same name, (possibly the persons who had given the name to the settlement). Some of this family had been acquainted with the now widely-known Mr. Solomon Spaulding, and from them Hurlburt learned that that gentleman had once written a romance called the "Manuscript Found," which professed to recount the history of the ancient inhabitants of this continent.

Hurlburt had now given himself up to the work of opposing "Mormonism." He quickly perceived that this romance could be used as a weapon to carry on the warfare. If he could obtain possession of it and find any points in common between it and the Book of Mormon he could exaggerate those seeming resemblances and falsify other statements. If he found no agreement between the two he could contrive to have the "Manuscript Found" accidentally (?) destroyed and then claim that its contents were almost identical with the record of Mormon. He found it necessary to pursue the latter course.

In carrying out his design he repaired to Kirtland, and there made an appointment to deliver a lecture, calling upon all who were opposed to "Mormonism" to attend. They did so in force. At this lecture Hurlburt told his audience that in his travels in the State of Pennsylvania, lecturing against "Mormonism," he had learned that one Mr. Spaulding had written a romance, and the probability was that it had by some means fallen into the hands of Sidney Rigdon, and that he had transformed it into the Book of Mormon. Hurlburt further stated that he intended to write a book, and call it "Mormonism Unveiled," in which he would reveal the whole secret.

His anti-"Mormon" hearers were delighted. One mobocrat, a Campbellite, advanced the sum of $300 towards

the prosecution of the work.   Others contributed for the
same purpose, and Hurlburt, being thus provided with funds,
at once proceeded to hunt up the manuscript.

With this view he journeyed to New Salem or Conneaut
Ohio, the place where Mr. Spaulding formerly resided.
There he called a meeting and made known his intentions.
His harangues created quite a stir.   He told the same story
about the manuscript and Sidney Rigdon that he had told in
Kirtland.   The idea was new to his hearers, but as it was
something which was to destroy "Mormonism," they did not
object to it, and some helped him with more money.   He was
here advised to visit Mrs. Davison, formerly the wife of Mr.
Spaulding, who now resided at Monson, Massachusetts.   This
he determined to do.

It should here be mentioned that the gospel had already
been preached with considerable success in the neighborhood
of New Salem;   and though it was the place where the
"Manuscript Found" was written, the Spaulding story was
never dreamed of there until Hurlburt mentioned it.   But
it was too good a thing for those who had rejected the truth
to let pass.   It afforded them some slight excuse for not
receiving the doctrines of "Mormonism."   Such persons
clutched at it eagerly, as drowning men are said to grasp at
straws.   Nevertheless the work of the Lord did not stand still
in those parts.   Numbers were afterwards baptized in that
very section, so little effect had Hurlburt's fabrication upon
the minds of the people.

Hurlburt at once carried out the advice given to him by
his New Salem acquaintances.   He proceeded to Monson,
called on Mrs. Davison, and by representing his wishes in
his own unscrupulous and untruthful manner obtained from
her the writings of her former husband.   Further she told
him that there was a trunk somewhere in the state of New
York that also contained papers which he might have, if they
were found to suit his purpose, and according to the latest
version of the story it was from that trunk that Hurlburt
obtained the "Manuscript Found."

Mrs. Davison positively asserts that she gave Hurlburt
the original of the "Manuscript Found,'" either directly, or

through her order to Mr. Clark, and that he promised to publish it, which however he never did. He claimed that *it did not read as he expected*, or he found nothing that *would suit his purpose.* In this he for once undoubtedly told the truth. Quite lately, however, he has made the following affidavit.

"GIBSONBURG, OHIO,

January 10th, 1881.

"To all whom it may concern :

"In the year eighteen hundred and thirty-four (1834), I went from Geauga county, Ohio, to Monson, Hampden county, Mass., where I found Mrs. Davison, late widow of the Rev. Solomon Spaulding, late of Conneaut, Ashtabula county, Ohio. Of her I obtained a manuscript, supposing it to be the manuscript of the romance written by the said Solomon Spaulding, called the 'Manuscript Found,' which was reported to be the foundation of the 'Book of Mormon.' I did not examine the manuscript till I got home, when upon examination I found it to contain nothing of the kind, but being a manuscript upon an entirely different subject. This manuscript I left with E. D. Howe, of Painsville, Geauga county, Ohio, now Lake county, Ohio, with the understanding that when he had examined it he should return it to the widow. Said Howe says the manuscript was destroyed by fire, and further the deponent saith not.

(Signed)   "D. P. HURLBURT."

Mrs. Davison says Hurlburt obtained the "Manuscript Found." He, in the above, says it was nothing of the kind, but *was a manuscript upon an entirely different subject.* What was that subject? Hurlburt in his original statement says, (these are his own words,) "It is a romance, purporting to have been translated from the Latin, found on twenty-four rolls of parchment, in a cave, but written in modern style— giving a fabulous account of a ship being driven upon the American coast, while proceeding from Rome to Britain, a short time previous to the Christian era; this country then being inhabited by the Indians."

Such is his description of the manuscript he received. No wonder it did not suit his purpose. No work treating on the ancient inhabitants of America could be more unlike the

Book of Mormon than this. But Mrs. Davison says this was the original of the "Manuscript Found." We regard it altogether more probable that this was the plot of Mr. Spaulding's romance than the ten tribe version, which we consider to be a later invention, manufactured by some ignorant anti-"Mormon," who really imagined that the Book of Mormon conveyed that idea. We have nothing more than unauthenticated gossip for the assertion that Mr. Spaulding ever believed that the American Indians were of Israelitish descent. In fact, it is stated that during the later years of that gentleman's life he was strongly inclined to infidelity.

If the papers given to Hurlburt contained the "Manuscript Found," as stated by Mrs. Davison, we know what became of it, if we can believe D. P. Hurlburt. It was burned so that it might never be brought up to confront those who claim that in it is to be found the origin of the Book of Mormon. If Hurlburt did not receive it, Mrs. Davison must have retained it. Then what became of it? Solomon Spaulding's family could have no possible motive for not publishing it. To them it would have been a mine of wealth; at least they thought so, as evidenced by the agreement between Mrs. Davison and Hurlburt, that she was to have half of the profits accruing from its publication, as hereafter shown in her interview with Mr. Haven.

There is another fact that strongly bears out Mrs. Davison's statement. It is this, that it is highly improbable that Mr. Spaulding would write two entirely distinct and varying romances on the ancient inhabitants of America. We never hear of him writing more than one on this subject. If then the Roman story was not the "Manuscript," what was it? It certainly in many particulars agrees with the statements of those who profess to know something about Mr. Spaulding's writings. Both (if there were two) are said to have been written in the Latin language; both were found, supposedly, in a cave near Conneaut, Ohio. This is altogether unlikely. The evidence, we believe, to be overwhelming that Hurlburt did receive the "Manuscript Found," and not finding it what he wanted, he destroyed it or had it destroyed.

We have previously referred to the Jacksons of Jackson settlement, Pennsylvania, from whom Hurlburt first heard of Mr. Spaulding's writings. In justice to Mr. Jackson it must be stated that on one occasion Hurlburt called on him and asked him to sign a document which testified to the probability of Mr. Spaulding's manuscript having been converted into the Book of Mormon. This he indignantly refused to do. He had read both books and knew there was no likeness between them. He then and there stated that there was no agreement between the two; adding that Mr. Spaulding's manuscript was a very small work in the form of a novel, which said not one word about the children of Israel, but professed to give an account of a race of people who originated from the Romans, which Mr. Spaulding said he had translated from a Latin parchment that he had found. The Book of Mormon, Mr. Jackson continued, purports to be written by a branch of the house of Israel; it is written in a different style, and is altogether different. For this reason he refused to lend his name to the lie, and expressed his indignation and contempt at Hurlburt's base and wicked project to deceive the public.

Mr. Jackson's recollection of the plot of the "Manuscript Found" tallies exactly with Hurlburt's description of the contents of the manuscript he received from Mrs. Davison, and is confirmatory evidence of the truth of her statement, that she gave the work to Hurlburt. It is also the strongest kind of testimony in favor of the theory that Spaulding's romance had nothing Israelitish in its narrative, but was Roman from beginning to end, in detail, incident, language, writing, parchment and all.

To return to Hurlburt's work; those who were anxious that it should be published, discovered that it would be better that it should not appear in his name, his reputation having grown too bad. The manuscript was therefore sold to Mr. Howe of Painesville, Ohio, for $500 and was published by him. It did not prove a financial success, its circulation was but small. Mr. Howe eventually offered the copies at half price, but they would not sell even at that reduction. Hurlburt rapidly spent his ill-gotten gains in drink, and for many years bore a most undesirable reputation. He is now an old man, residing at Gibsonburg, Ohio.

The following remarks regarding D. P. Hurlburt, are from the writings of the late Elder Joseph E. Johnson.

"In the year A. D. 1833, then living in Kirtland, Ohio, I became acquainted with a man subsequently known as Dr. Hurlburt. He was a man of fine physique, very pompous, good looking and veriy ambitous, with some energy, though of poor education. Soon after his arrival he came to my mother's house to board, where he remained for nearly a year. While there he made an effort to get into a good practice of medicine, sought position in the Church, and was ever striving to make marital connection with any of the 'first families.'

"Finally in 1834, he was charged with illicit intercourse with the other sex; was tried and cut off the Church. He denied, expostulated, threatened. but of no use, the facts were too apparent, and he at once vowed himself the enemy of the Church—threatened to write a book that would annihilate 'Mormonism,' and went to Painesville, ten miles, and allied himself to a publisher there, who agreed to print his book if he would furnish the matter. A fund was raised by the anti-"Mormons" in the village around, and enough means raised to send Hurlburt east to hunt up and obtain the writings of Solomon Spaulding, called the 'Manuscript Found', which had already become famous as the alleged matter from which the Book of Mormon was written.

"Hurlburt went east and was absent some two or three months—and on his return publicly declared that *he could not obtain it*, but instead brought several affidavits from persons who claimed to have heard Solomon Spaulding read his 'Manuscript Found' in 1812, and believed, as well as they could remember, that the matter and story were the same as printed in the Book of Mormon. And these were published in his book of 'Mormonism Exposed,' in that or the subsequent year, but not a sentence from the 'Manuscript Found,' which it appears that *he did really obtain*, but finding no similarity between the two, suppressed the Spaulding manuscript, while he publicly announced in his book that he had entirely failed to obtain it. Hurlburt proved himself to be a man of gross immorality and was untruthful and unreliable."

CHAPTER III.

THE BOGUS AFFIDAVIT.

THE next noteworthy person who entered upon the crusade against the Book of Mormon was a Congregationalist minister of Holliston, Massachusetts, named Storrs.

This man was greatly annoyed at the loss of some of the best members of his congregation through the preaching of the everlasting gospel, and in his anger published to the world what he asserted was the affidavit of the widow of Solomon Spaulding, but which she afterwards repudiated, as shown from the following article published in the Quincy (Illinois) *Whig* shortly after the appearance of the bogus affidavit:

"A CUNNING DEVICE DETECTED.

"It will be recollected that a few months since an article appeared in several of the papers, purporting to give an account of the origin of the Book of Mormon. How far the writer of that piece has effected his purposes, or what his purposes were in pursuing the course he has, I shall not attempt to say at this time, but shall call upon every candid man to judge in this matter for himself, and shall content myself by presenting before the public the other side of the question in the form of a letter, as follows:

"Copy of a letter written by Mr. John Haven, of Holliston, Middlesey Co., Massachusetts, to his daughter, Elizabeth Haven, of Quincy, Adams Co., Illinois.

"Your brother Jesse passed through Monson, where he saw Mrs Davison and her daughter, Mrs. McKinstry, and also Dr. Ely, and spent several hours with them, during which time he asked them the following questions, viz. :

Question.—'Did you, Mrs. Davison, write a letter to John Storrs, giving an account of the origin of the Book of Mormon?'

Answer.—'I did not.'

Q.—'Did you sign your name to it?'

A.—'I did not, neither did I ever see the letter until I saw it in the *Boston Recorder*, the letter was never brought to me to sign.'

Q.—'What agency had you in having this letter sent to Mr. Storrs?'

A.—'D. R. Austin came to my house and asked me some questions, took some minutes on paper, and from these minutes wrote that letter.'

Q.—'Have you read the Book of Mormon?'

A.—'I have read some in it.'

Q.—'Does Mr. Spaulding's manuscript and the Book of Mormon agree?'

A.—'I think some few of the names are alike.'

Q.—'Does the manuscript describe an idolatrous or a religious people?'

Q.—'An idolatrous people.'

A.—'Where is the manuscript?'

A.—'D. P. Hurlburt came here and took it, said he would get it printed and let me have one half of the profits.'

Q.—'Has D. P. Hurlburt got the manuscript printed?'

A.—'I received a letter stating that it did not read as he expected, and he should not print it.'

Q.—'How large is Mr. Spaulding's manuscript?'

A.—'About one-third as large as the Book of Mormon.'

Q.—To Mrs. McKinstry: 'How old were you when your father wrote the manuscript?'

A.—'About five years of age.'

Q.—'Did you ever read the manuscript?'

A.—'When I was about twelve years old I used to read it for diversion.'

Q.—'Did the manuscript describe an idolatrous or a religious people?'

A.—'An idolatrous people.'

Q.—'Does the manuscript and the Book of Mormon agree?'

A.—'I think some of the names agree.'

Q.—'Are you certain that some of the names agree?'

A.—'I am not.'

Q.—'Have you read any in the Book of Mormon?'

A.—'I have not.'

Q.—'Was your name attached to that letter, which was sent to Mr. John Storrs, by your order?'

A.—'No, I never meant that my name should be there.'

'You see by the above questions and answers, that Mr. Austin, in his great zeal to destroy the Latter-day Saints, has asked Mrs. Davison a few questions, then wrote a letter to Mr.

Storrs in his own language. I do not say that the above questions and answers were given in the form that I have written them, but these questions were asked, and these answers given. Mrs. Davison is about seventy years of age, and somewhat broke.'

"This may certify that I am personally acquainted with Mr. Haven, his son and daughter, and am satisfied they are persons of truth. I have also read Mr. Haven's letter to his daughter, which has induced me to copy it for publication, and I further say, the above is a correct copy of Mr. Haven's letter.

A. BADLAM."

Notwithstanding the above refutation and *expose* the opponents of "Mormonism" have continually from the time of its publication, copied, re-published and harped upon this forged affidavit of Mrs. Davison. Their ears have been ever deaf and their eyes blind when the refutation of the slander has been presented to them. They did not then, and do not now want it; they prefer the lie which one of their number has concocted and spread broad-cast through the world.

We must now turn to Sidney Rigdon who by many is regarded as the agent or go-between by and through whom Joseph Smith came into possession of the "Manuscript Found," and who was, in fact, the chief instrument in converting that romance into the Book of Mormon. It is urged that Joseph had neither the learning, ability nor industry to perform so arduous a literary work, but that Rigdon had the audacity, cunning and education necessary to perpetrate such a fraud, and that Joseph Smith was his willing tool, whom he used as a screen to protect himself from public observation and through whom he palmed his imposture on the world. None of those who accept this theory have yet been able to explain what possible motive Rigdon could have had in taking such a course, were such an arrangement possible; but we have most trustworthy and reliable testimony that it could not be so for two altogether sufficient reasons:

First: Sidney Rigdon never was at Pittsburg or any other place at the same time as Mr. Spaulding's manuscript was there and therefore he could not have seen or read it, it being remembered that it never was out of the possession of the

author's family only during the short time it is said to have
been in the hands of Mr. Patterson.

Second: Sidney Rigdon never saw Joseph Smith until years
after the latter received the sacred plates, indeed, not until
after the Book of Mormon had been printed and the Church
of Jesus Christ organized.

Let us consider the first of the above propositions. Mr.
Spaulding resided in Pittsburg only for a short time between
1812, when he lived at Conneaut, and 1816 when he died a
Amity. The general opinion is that he moved to the last
named place in 1814. It was then, between 1812 and 1814,
that, if ever, the manuscript was in the hands of Mr. Patterson; Sidney Rigdon was then a youth of not more than twenty
years of age, residing on and working his deceased father's farm
at St. Clair, Pennsylvania. To make this point more clear,
we will here give a short sketch of Rigdon's early life:

Sidney Rigdon was born in St. Clair township, Alleghany
Co., Pa., on the 19th of February, 1793. In his twenty-fifth
year he connected himself with a society, which in that country
was called Regular Baptists. In March, 1819, he received a
license to preach in that society, and in the following May he
left Pennsylvania and went to Trumbull Co., Ohio, where he
was afterwards married. In 1821 he was called to the pastoral
charge of the first Baptist church of Pittsburg, which invita-
tion he accepted early in the following year, and soon became a
popular minister. After ministering in that position for two
and a half years he withdrew from that sect, because he considered its doctrines were not altogether in accord with the scriptures. With Mr. Alexander Campbell he founded the "Campbellite" or "Disciples" church; but having retired from the
ministry he for two years worked as a day laborer in a tannery;
after which he removed to Bainbridge, Geauga Co., Ohio,
where the people solicited him to preach. He complied with
their request and soon grew quite popular. He
advocated the doctrines of repentance and baptism for the
remission of sins, and baptized numbers from all the country
round. During this time he removed from Bainbridge to
Mentor, some thirty miles distant, and it was there that Parley
P. Pratt and other Elders found him, in the Fall of 1830.

We will now give the testimony of a number of persons who were most intimately acquainted with Sidney Rigdon during his youth. These testimonies we copy from a work lately published by Mr. Robert Patterson, of Pittsburg, son of Mr. Patterson, the printer, to whom the Spaulding romance is said to have been taken. He is the person called "the present writer" in these extracts, which in his work follow a short account of Sidney's early life:

"1. Rigdon's relatives at Library, Pa., Carvil Rigdon (his brother) and Peter Boyer (his brother-in-law), in a written statement dated Jan. 27th, 1843, certify to the facts and dates as above stated in regard to his birth, schooling, uniting with the church, licensure, ordination and settlement in Pittsburg in 1822. Mr. Boyer also in a personal interview with the present writer in 1879 positively affirmed that Rigdon had never lived in Pittsburg previous to 1822, adding that they were boys together and he ought to know. Mr. Boyer had for a short time embraced Mormonism, but became convinced that it was a delusion and returned to his membership in the Baptist church.

"2. Isaac King, a highly-respected citizen of Library, Pa., and an old neighbor of Rigdon, states in a letter to the present writer, dated June 14th, 1879, that Sidney lived on the farm of his father until the death of the latter, in May, 1810, and for a number of years afterwards, farming with very indifferent success; 'it was said he was too lazy and proud to make a good farmer;' received his education in a log school-house in the vicinity; 'began to talk in public on religion soon after his admission to the church, probably at his own instance, as there is no record of his licensure;' went to Sharon, Pa., for a time, and was there ordained as a preacher, but soon returned to his farm, which he sold (June 28th, 1823) to James Means, and about the time of sale removed to Pittsburg.

"3. Samuel Cooper, of Saltsburg, Pa., a veteran of three wars, in a letter to the present writer, dated June 14th, 1879, stated as follows: 'I was acquainted with Mr. Lambdin, was often in the printing-office; was acquainted with Silas Engles, the foreman of the printing-office; he never mentioned Sidney Rigdon's name to me, so I am satisfied he was never engaged there as a printer. I was introduced to Sidney Rigdon in 1843; he stated to me that he was a Mormon preacher or lecturer; 1 was acquainted with him during 1843–45; never knew him before, and never knew him as a printer; never saw him in the book-store or printing-office; your father's office was in the celebrated Molly Murphy's Row."

"4.   Rev. Robert P. Du Bois, of New London, Pa., under date of Jan. 9th, 1879, writes: 'I entered the book-store of R. Patterson & Lambdin in March, 1818, when about twelve years old, and remained there until the Summer of 1820. The firm had under its control a book-store on Fourth Street, a book-bindery, a printing-office (not newspaper, but job-office, under the name of Butler & Lambdin), entrance on Diamond Alley, and a steam paper-mill on the Allegheny (under the name of R. & J. Patterson).   I knew nothing of Spaulding (then dead) or of his book, or of Sidney Rigdon.''

"5.   Mrs. R. W. Lambdin, of Irvington, N. Y., widow of the late J. Harrison Lambdin, in response to some inquiries as to her recollection of Rigdon and others, writes under date of Jan. 15th, 1882: 'I am sorry to say I shall not be able to give you any information relative to the persons you name.   They certainly could not have been friends of Mr. Lambdin.' Mrs. Lambdin resided in Pittsburg from her marriage in 1819, to the death of her husband, Aug. 1st, 1825.   Mr. Lambdin was born Sep. 1st, 1798.''

In addition to this we have the testimony of Sidney Rigdon's mother.   She informed one gentleman, who published her statement years ago, long before the Spaulding story was concocted, and therefore with no design to mislead on that matter, that her son lived at home and worked on the farm until the twenty-sixth year of his age; and was never engaged in public life until after that period, either politically or religiously.   Thus, according to his mother's statement which is sustained by these other testimonies, he did not leave home until 1819.   He did not go to Pittsburg until 1822; eight or nine years after the manuscript of Spaulding's romance had been returned to its author (if, indeed, it had ever been out of his hands), and that author had removed from Pittsburg and died.

Again it is asserted that Sidney Rigdon was associated with the printing-office of Patterson and Lambdin during his stay in Pittsburg. The testimony above given is very strong evidence to the contrary. In addition to which we have Rigdon's own refutation of the falsehood, made at the time that Mrs. Davison's bogus affidavit was first given to the world. He asserts in effect, most positively, that when he went to Pittsburg he did so as a minister of the gospel at the call of a religious congregation, and was never in any way directly or indirectly connected with any printing office during his stay there; and if he had been associated with a Pittsburg printing office nobody claims that the "Manuscript Found" was in that city at that late date (1822). According to Mrs. McKinstry's already quoted affidavit it was then hid up in an old trunk at a small village called Hardwicks, in the state of New York, hundreds of miles from Pittsburg. To tide over this difficulty some one has suggested that probably Spaulding made a copy of his romance for the printer, and it was this copy that Rigdon afterwards found. But this is a baseless supposition; until lately such an idea was never thought of, and it loses all its force from the fact that those best acquainted with the history of that manuscript say that the copy Spaulding gave to Patterson was returned to him; it was not left in the office to be found by Rigdon, or any one else in after years.

It may be asked, is there no conflicting testimony? Do not some persons assert that Rigdon was in Pittsburg and acquainted with Patterson and Lambdin years before 1822? Yes, but their testimony is of little value for many reasons. It is, in the first place, almost invariably second hand. They do not testify of what they themselves actually knew on these points, but of what somebody else knew, or said, or told them. In the second place, they are made, as a rule, by very aged persons, whose memory, when we consider the mass of trash that has been published on this subject, cannot be trusted. They, where desiring to be truthful, have mixed up what they really knew and what they have since heard and read. A third class are "divines," men with "reverend" tacked on their names, whose testimony, it is a sad fact but it is a truth, can scarcely ever be trusted on anything pertaining to "Mormonism." One

very aged lady, whose father and husband kept the post office
from 1804 to 1833, says that Rigdon and Lambdin used to come
together to the post office for mail matter as early as 1815, if
not earlier, and that as youths they were very intimate. But
it must be remembered that there was a difference of six or
seven years in the ages of these two young men, Rigdon
being the elder, and Mr. Lambdin's wife asserts of him and
others that "they certainly could not have been friends of Mr.
Lambdin." Again it is altogether inconsistent to believe that a
young man of Rigdon's ambition would associate with a boy so
many years his junior; the supposition is altogether more consistent that this lady has mixed her names and dates, and that young
Lambdin having a companion who came with him for letters,
she has in the course of many years confused this companion
with Rigdon who doubtless often visited the post office at a
later period, and at a time when his name would be well known
through all Pittsburg.

But it is an open question whether Mr. Patterson ever had
the "Manuscript Found" in his possession. The Spaulding
family say that he had, he asserts that he had not. On being
interrogated on the subject, soon after the publication of
Mrs. Davison's bogus affidavit, he said that he knew nothing
of any such manuscript.* Even Hurlburt states that "he
called on Mr. Patterson who affirmed *his entire ignorance of
the whole matter.*" Here is evidently a grand mistake or a
gross falsehood. To us, it seems from the evidence, that the
story of Mr. Patterson having received the manuscript was first
invented by Priest Storrs on purpose to connect Sidney Rigdon
with the "Manuscript Found" and the ladies of the Spaulding
family have heard it so often reiterated that in their old age they
have imagined that they have some recollection of such an
incident, when, in truth, it is only the confused remembrance
of what has been ding-donged into their ears by over-anxious
opponents of "Mormonism" for the last forty years. It is a
well-known fact that the human mind is so constituted that
after brooding over imaginary circumstances for a lengthened

---

*——The gentleman to whom he made this statement is under-
stood to have been Mr. Ephraim S. Green, of Philadelphia.

period it will frequently grow to regard such fables as facts. This peculiarity of the human mind has often been commented upon. A laughable incident in this connection is related regarding King George IV., of England. He got it into his head that he was present at the battle of Waterloo, and was especially fond of referring to the circumstance in the presence of the Duke of Wellington, and then requiring the aged warrior to back up his statement. It is said that the duke, with the true instinct of the courtier, would reply on such occasions, "I have heard your majesty mention that circumstance before." So Mrs. Davison and her daughter have so frequently heard the statement that the Book of Mormon was taken from the "Manuscript Found," that the "Manuscript Found" related to the lost ten tribes, that Mr. Patterson borrowed it in Pittsburg, and that Sidney Rigdon had something inexplicable to do with it, that these ladies actually came to believe that these assertions were all truths, and in their old age were willing to make affidavit to their belief in many things about which in earlier days they were nothing like so sure.

With regard to the second point, as to when Joseph Smith first saw Sidney Rigdon, we draw attention to the two following extracts from the writings of Elder Parley P. Pratt:

"THE MORMONITES.

"To the Editor of the New York Era :

"Sir.—In yours of the 20th inst., there is an article copied from the *Boston Recorder*, headed, 'Mormon Bible,' and signed, 'Matilda Davison,' which, justice to our society and to the public requires me to answer, and I trust that a sense of justice will induce you, sir, to give your readers both sides of the question.

"I am one of the society who believe the Book of Mormon, and as such I am assailed in the statement professing to come from Matilda Davison.

"In the first place, there is no such thing in existence as the 'Mormon Bible.' The 'Mormons,' as they are vulgarly called, believe in the same Bible that all Christendom profess to believe in, viz.: the common version of the Old and New Testament. The Book of Mormon is not entitled a Bible, except by those who misrepresent it. It is entitled the 'Book of Mormon.'

"The religious sect alluded to in your paper, are there accused of knavery and superstition. Now we are not sensible of being guilty of knavery, and we do not know wherein we are superstitious, but very much desire to know in order that we may reform. If some good minister or editor will condescend to particulars and point out our superstitions, we will take it as a great kindness, for we are the declared enemies to knavery and superstition.

"If a firm believer in the gospel of a crucified and risen Redeemer, as manifested to all nations, and as recorded in their sacred books, amounts to superstition, then we are superstitious. If preaching that system to others and calling them to repentance is superstition, then we are superstitious. If refusing to fellowship the modern systems of sectarianism which are contrary to the pure doctrines of the Bible be superstition, then we are superstitious, for we hereby declare our withdrawal from all the mysticism, priestcraft and superstitions, and from all the creeds, doctrines, commandments, traditions and precepts of men, as far as they are contrary to the ancient faith and doctrine of the Saints; and we hereby bear our testimony against them.

"We do not believe that God ever instituted more than one religious system under the same dispensation, therefore we do not admit that two different sects can possibly be right. The Churches of Jesus Christ, in any age or country, must be all built upon the same faith, the same baptism, the same Lord, the same Holy Spirit, which would guide them into all truth, and consequently from all error and superstition. The Book of Mormon has never been placed by us in the place of the sacred scriptures, but, as before said, the sacred scriptures stand in their own place, and the Book of Mormon abundantly corroborates and bears testimony of the truth of the Bible. Indeed there is no society, within our knowledge, whose members adhere more closely to the Bible than ours. For proof of this we appeal to the multitudes who attend our religious meetings in this city and in all other places.

"The piece in your paper states that 'Sidney Rigdon was connected in the printing office of Mr. Patterson' (in Pittsburg), and that 'this is a fact well known in that region, and as Rigdon himself has frequently stated. Here he had ample opportunity to become acquainted with Mr. Spaulding's manuscript (romance) and to copy it if he chose.' This statement is utterly and entirely false. Mr. Rigdon was never connected with the said printing establishment, either directly or indirectly, and we defy the world to bring proof of any such connection. Now the person or persons who fabricated that falsehood would do well to repent and become persons of truth and veracity before they express such acute sensibility concerning the religious pretensions of others. The statement that Sidney Rigdon is one of the founders of the said religious sect is also incorrect.

"The sect was founded in the state of New York, while
Mr. Rigdon resided in Ohio, several hundred miles distant.
Mr. Rigdon embraced the doctrine through my instrument-
ality. I first presented the Book of Mormon to him. I stood
upon the bank of the stream while he was baptized, and
assisted to officiate in his ordination, and I myself was unacquainted with the system until some months after its organization, which was on the 6th of April, 1830, and I embraced
it in September following.

"The piece further states that 'a woman preacher appointed
a meeting at New Salem, Ohio, and in the meeting read and
repeated copious extracts from the Book of Mormon.' Now,
it is a fact well known, that we have not had a female preacher
in our connection, for we do not believe in a female priesthood.
It further says that the excitement in New Salem became so
great that the inhabitants had a meeting and deputed Doctor
Philastus Hurlburt, one of their members, to repair to
Spaulding's widow, and obtain from her the original manuscript of the romance, etc. But the statement does not say
whether he obtained the manuscript, but still leaves the
impression that he did, and that it was compared with the
Book of Mormon. Now who ever will read the work got up
by said Hulburt, entitled: 'Mormonism Unveiled,' will find
that he there states that the said manuscript of Spaulding's
romance was lost and could nowhere be found. But the
widow is here made to say that it is carefully preserved. Here
seems to be some knavery or crooked work; and no wonder,
for this said Hurlburt is one of the most notorious rascals in
the western country. He was first cut off from our society
for an attempt at seduction and crime, and secondly he was
laid under bond in Geauga county, Ohio, for threatening to
murder Joseph Smith, Jr., after which he laid a deep design
of the Spaulding romance imposition, in which he has been
backed by evil and designing men in different parts of the
country, and sometimes by those who do not wish to do wrong,
but who are ignorant on the subject. Now what but falsehood could be expected from such a person? Now if there is
such a manuscript in existence, let it come forward at once
and not be kept in the dark. Again, if the public will be
patient, they will doubtless find that the piece signed 'Matilda
Davison' (Spaulding's widow) is a base fabrication by Priest
Storrs, of Holliston, Mass., in order to save his craft, after
losing the deacon of his church, and several of its most pious
and intelligent members, who left his society to embrace what
they considered to be truth. At any rate, a judge of
literary productions, who can swallow that piece of writing as
the production of a women in private life, can be made to

believe that the book of Mormon is a romance. For the one is as much like a romance as the other is like a woman's composition.

"The production signed 'Matilda Davison,' is evidently the work of a man accustomed to public address, and the Book of Mormon I know to be true, and the Spaulding story, as far as the Book of Mormon is connected with it, I know to be false.

"I now leave the subject with a candid public, with a sincere desire that those who have been deluded with such vain and foolish lies, may be undeceived.

"Editors, who have given publicity to the Spaulding story, will do an act of justice by giving publicity to the foregoing.

"P. P. PRATT.

"New York, Nov. 27th, 1839."

The following explicit statement is also copied from the earlier writings of Elder Parley P. Pratt:

"About A. D. 1827, Messrs. A. Campbell, W. Scott, and S. Rigdon, with some others, residing in Virginia, Ohio, etc., came off from the Baptist, and established a new order, under the name of Reformed Baptist, or Disciples. And they were termed by their enemies, Campbellites, Rigdonites, etc. This reformation as to its doctrine, consisted principally of the baptism of repentance, for the remission of sins, etc. And Mr. Rigdon in particular held to a literal fulfillment, and application of the written word, and by this means he was an instrument to turn many from the false notions of sectarianism, to an understanding of the prophecies, touching the great restoration of Israel, and the mighty revolutions of the last days. Many hundred disciples were gathered by his ministry, throughout the lake country of Ohio, and many other preachers stood in connection with him in these principles. I was then pursuing agricultural life, and mostly occupied in converting the wilderness into a fruitful field. But being a member of the Baptist church, and a lover of truth, I became acquainted with Mr. Rigdon, and a believer in, and teacher of the same doctrine. After proclaiming those principles in my own neighborhood, and the adjoining country, I at length took a journey to the state of New York, partly on a visit to Columbia county, N. Y., my native place, and partly for the purpose of ministering the word. This journey was undertaken in August, 1830; I had no sooner reached Ontario county, N. Y., than I came in contact with the Book of Mormon, which had then been published about six months, and had gathered about fifty disciples, which were all who then constituted the church of Latter-day Saints. I was greatly prejudiced against the book, but remembering the caution of Paul, 'Prove all things, hold fast that which is good,' I sat down to read it, and after carefully comparing it with the other scriptures, and praying to God, He gave me the knowledge of its truth, by the power of the Holy Ghost, and what was I, that I could withstand God? I accordingly obeyed the ordinances and was commissioned by revelation, and the laying on of hands, to preach the fulness of the gospel. Then, after finishing my visit to Columbia county, I returned to the brethren in Ontario county, where, for the first time, I saw Mr. Joseph Smith, Jr., who had just returned from Pennsylvania to his father's house in Manchester. About the 15th of October, 1830, I took my journey in company with Elders O. Cowdery and Peter Whitmer, to Ohio. We called on Elder S. Rigdon, and then for the first time his eyes beheld the Book of Mormon, I, myself, had the happiness to present it to him in person. He was much surprised, and it was with much persuasion and argument, that he was prevailed on to read it, and after he had read it, he had a great struggle of mind, before he fully believed, and embraced it; and when finally convinced of its truth, he called together a large congregation of his friends, neighbors and brethren, and then addressed them very affectionately for nearly two hours during most of which time, both himself and nearly all the congregation were melted into tears. He asked forgiveness of everybody who might have had occasion to be offended with any part of his former life; he forgave all who had persecuted or injured him in any manner, and the next morning, himself and wife were baptized by Elder O. Cowdery. I was present, it was a solemn scene, most of the people were greatly affected, they came out of the water overwhelmed in tears. Many others were baptized by us in that vicinity, both before and after his baptism, insomuch that during the Fall of 1830, and the following Winter and Spring, the number of the disciples was increased to about one thousand, the Holy Ghost was mightily poured out, and the word of God grew and multiplied, and many priests were obedient to the faith. Early in 1831, Mr. Rigdon having been ordained under our hands, visited Elder J. Smith, Jr., in the state of New York, for the first time, and from that time forth rumor began to circulate that he, Rigdon, was the author of the Book of Mormon.

"The Spaulding story never was dreamed of until several years afterwards, when it appeared in 'Mormonism Unveiled'—a base forgery, by D. P. Hurlburt and others of similar character, who strove to account for the Book of Mormon in some other way than the truth. In the west, whole neighborhoods embraced Mormonism, after this fable of the Spaulding story had been circulated among them: indeed, we never considered it worthy of an answer, until it was converted, by the ignorant and impudent religious editors of this city, into something said to be positively certain, and not to be disputed. Now, I testify that the forgers of the Spaulding lie (concerning S. Rigdon and others), are of the same description as those who forged the lie against the disciples of old, accusing them of stealing the body of Jesus, etc."

We also insert, at this point, the affidavit of the only surviving sister of Joseph Smith, which conclusively shows that Sidney Rigdon had no communication with the Prophet or any other of the family until months after the Book of Mormon was published.

"STATE OF ILLINOIS, } ss.
     Kendall county.

"I. Katherine Salisbury, being duly sworn, depose and say, ·that I am a resident of the state of Illinois, and have been for forty years last past; that I will be sixty-eight years of age, July 28th, 1881.

That I am a daughter of Joseph Smith, Senior, and sister to Joseph Smith, Jr., the translator of the Book of Mormon. That at the time the said book was published, I was seventeen years of age; that at the time of the publication of said book, my brother, Joseph Smith, Jr., lived in the family of my father, in the town of Manchester, Ontario county, New York, and that he had, all of his life to this time made his home with the family.

"That at the time, and for years prior thereto, I lived in and was a member of such family, and personally knowing to the things transacted in said family, and those who visited at my father's house, and the friends of the family, and the friends and acquaintances of my brother, Joseph Smith, Jr., who visited at or came to my father's house.

"That prior to the latter part of the year A. D. 1830, there was no person who visited with, or was an acquaintance of, or called upon the said family, or any member thereof to my knowledge, by the name of Sidney Rigdon; nor was such person known to the family, or any member thereof, to my knowledge, until the last part of the year A. D. 1830, or the first part of the year 1831, and some time after the organization of the Church of Jesus Christ, by Joseph Smith, Jr., and several months after the publication of the Book of Mormon.

"That I remember the time when Sidney Rigdon came to my father's place, and that it was after the removal of my father from Waterloo, N. Y., to Kirtland, Ohio. That this was in the year 1831, and some months after the publication of the Book of Mormon, and fully one year after the Church was organized, as before stated herein.

"That I make this statement, not on account of fear, favor, or hope of reward of any kind; but simply that the truth may be known with reference to said matter, and that the foregoing statements made by me are true, as I verily believe.

"KATHERINE SALISBURY.

"Sworn before me, and subscribed in my presence, by the said Katherine Salisbury, this 15th day of April, A. D. 1881.

"J. H. JENKS, *Notary Public.*"

Has it ever entered into the thoughts of our opponents that if Sidney Rigdon was the author or adapter of the Book of Mormon how vast and wide spread must have been the conspiracy that foisted it upon the world! Whole families must have been engaged in it. Men of all ages and various conditions in life, and living in widely separate portions of the country must have been connected with it. First we must include in the catalogue of conspirators the whole of the Smith family, then the Whitmer's, Martin Harris and Oliver Cowdery; further, to carry out this absurd idea, Sidney Rigdon and Parley P. Pratt must have been their active fellow-conspirators in arranging, carrying out and consummating their iniquitous fraud. To do this they must have traveled thousands of miles and spent months, perhaps years, to accomplish—what? That is the unsolved problem. Was it for the purpose of duping the world? They, at any rate the great majority of them, were of all men most unlikely to be engaged in such a folly. Their habits, surroundings, station in life, youth and inexperience all forbid such a thought. What could they gain, in any light that could be then presented to their minds, by palming such a deception upon the world? This is another unanswerable question. Then comes the staggering fact, if the Book be a falsity, that all these families, all these diverse characters, in all the trouble, perplexity, persecution and suffering through which they passed, never wavered in their testimony, never changed their statements, never "went back" on their original declarations, but continued unto death (and they have all passed away save a very few), proclaiming that the Book of Mormon was a divine revelation, and that its record was true. Was there ever such an exhibition in the history of the world of such continued, such unabating, such undeviating falsehood? if falsehood it was. We cannot find a place in the annals of their lives where they wavered, and what makes the matter more remarkable is that it can be said of most of them, as is elsewhere said of the three witnesses, they became offended with the Prophet Joseph, and a number of them openly rebelled against him ; but they never retracted one word with regard to the genuineness of Mormon's inspired record.   Whether they were friends or foes to Joseph, whether they regarded him as God's continued mouthpiece or as a fallen Prophet, they still persisted in their statements with regard to the book and the veracity of their earlier testimonies.   How can we possibly with our knowledge of human nature make this undeviating, unchanging, unwavering course, continuing over fifty years consistent with a deliberate, premeditated and cunningly-devised and executed fraud!

CHAPTER IV.

MRS. DICKENSON'S SPECULATIONS.

WE next invite attention to one of the latest versions of the "Spaulding story." It appeared in *Scribner's Magazine* for August, 1880, and purports to be written by Mrs. Ellen E. Dickenson, a grand-niece of Mr. Spaulding.   It is conspicuous for its inexactness, but is valuable as containing the affidavit of Mrs. M. S. McKinstry already considered.

Referring to the discovery by Mr. Spaulding of bows and other relics in a mound near his home at Conneaut, Mrs. Dickenson writes:

"This discovery suggested to him the subject for a new romance, which he called a translation from some *hieroglyphical writing* exhumed from the mound.   This romance purported to be a history of the peopling of America by the *lost tribes of Israel*, the tribes and their leaders *having very singular names*, among them Mormon, Moroni, Lamanite, Nephi.   The romance the author called 'Manuscript Found.' This all occurred in 1812, when to write a book was a distinction, and Mr. Spaulding read his manuscript from time to time to a circle of *admiring friends*.   He determined finally to publish it and for that purpose carried it to Pittsburg, Pennsylvania, to a printer by the name of Patterson. After keeping it awhile, Mr. Patterson returned it, declining to print it. *There was at this time in this printing office a young man named Sidney Rigdon*, who twenty years later figured as a preacher among the Saints."

In the above extract we have printed in italics those statements to which we wish to draw special attention.

Mrs. Dickenson says Mr. Spaulding called his romance "a translation from some hieroglyphical writing." This is an entirely new version of the old fiction. According to the original story it was written in Latin, but now after fifty years the writing is changed to hieroglyphics to make the theory agree better with the Book of Mormon which was translated from plates engraved in reformed Egyptian. We are told by earlier writers, before the matter was so entirely befogged as it is now by anti-"Mormon" speculations, assumptions and hypothesis, that the author's idea was to palm off his romance as a reality, and when he wrote it he expected the masses would believe it when published. Now it would be quite consistent for a graduate of Dartmouth College (as was Mr. Spaulding) to translate a Latin parchment—that would appear to be an every-day matter for a recognized clergyman of an orthodox sect, but to translate hieroglyphics would be entirely another thing; for it must not be forgotten that it was not until nearly thirty years after Mr. Spaulding wrote his "Manuscript Found" that the first dictionary and first grammar of Egyptian hieroglyphics were published.* Egyptiology being now a science, Mrs. Dickenson has outraged all consistency by claiming that Mr. Spaulding pretended to translate from hieroglyphics of which none at that time had any definite understanding. Mr. Spaulding as an educated man who wished his work to receive credence would know better than to start off with an evident, tell-tale impossibility.

Mrs. Dickenson calls the names in the Book of Mormon "very singular." This is because she has not read the book. A large number of the names in Mormon's sacred record are also found in the Holy Bible; as examples: Jacob, Joseph, Aaron, Noah, Jeremiah, Isaiah, Ishmael, Lemuel, Timothy,

---

*———Those of M. Champolleon published between 1836 and 1844.

Shem, etc. Are these singular? Another large percentage finish with the Hebrew termination: iah (Jah) an abbreviation of Jehovah. One scribbler asserts that "the real author of the Book of Mormon was well acquainted with the classics; the names of most of his heroes have the Latin termination of i, such as Nephi, Lehi, Moroni." This ignoramus was evidently not himself acquainted with the classics or he would have known that the most frequent termination of the masculine singular in the Latin language is *us* not i; and of names ending in *us* there are but very few in the Book of Mormon, probably half a dozen. Mrs. Dickenson gives an example of some of these "singular names:" "Mormon, Moroni, Lamanite and Nephi." Surely neither Laman or Moroni are singular names. There are, at any rate, more than one river of this name in South America running through the region where, according to Book of Mormon history, the Nephite general, Moroni, carried on his campaigns and held military control. Nephi is an ancient Egyptian name, and a title of Osiris, one of the gods of that people; its meaning is "the benevolent one." That it was common among the Israelites of the age of Nephi (B. C. 600) is shown from the fact that the word Nephites in the original Hebrew plural form occurs twice in the Bible, in Ezra ii., 50, and Nehemiah vii., 52. Lehi is also a Bible proper name.

Regarding the circle of "admiring friends" who heard the "Manuscript Found" read by its author, is it not a little singular that they so loudly praised it when the Book of Mormon, which is said to have been copied from it "word for word," is berated as uninteresting, dull, dry, stupid and everything else that is not commended or admired in literary productions? Neither is the style of the Book of Mormon that of a man educated in modern English; it is incomprehensible that a student in the literature of this age would express himself in the phraseology and style of this record. And again it is not written in the language of either Joseph Smith or Sidney Rigdon. If we compare the revelations given through Joseph Smith at the time the plates were being translated, we find an altogether different diction; or let us compare it with the Lectures on Faith in the Book of Doctrine and Covenants and then with the acknowledged writings of Sidney Rigdon, and we shall find there is nothing common in any of these with the peculiarities of grammatical construction and verbal idiosyncracies of the Book of Mormon. Judging then by the usual and accepted methods of criticism on which some rely so strongly, and throwing out the direct evidence as to its origin, this book could not be the creation of either Solomon Spaulding, Sidney Rigdon or Joseph Smith. Again, how is it that when the manuscript of the Book of Mormon was presented to the printer (see Mr. Gilbert's statement) it was misspelled and without punctuation. Did neither the graduate of Dartmouth College nor the minister of a flourishing religious congregation, who, by the way, according to some accounts, had formerly worked in a printing office, know anything of punctuation? This is the extreme of folly. But if they did, what conceivable reason could there be for leaving the punctuation out of the copy taken to the printer. Mr. Gilbert's statement of the great care shown by Hyrum Smith to have the book printed exactly as written, his extreme solicitude regarding the manuscript, his ignorance of the use of commas, colons, etc., and his one unwavering and unchanging testimony regarding the discovery and translation of the plates are all strong corroborative evidence that no educated man had anything to do with the production of the book; and how inconsistent with the stories of Joseph Smith's confirmed laziness is the idea that he would go to the trouble of copying out a manuscript which makes more than six hundred pages of closely printed matter! The promoters of the "Spaulding story" are terribly inconsistent in the various parts of their theory.

The statement that Mr. Spaulding took his romance to Mr. Patterson may be true or it may not, individually we do not believe it, but the assertion that Sidney Rigdon worked in that gentleman's printing office we have elsewhere shown to be utterly false. We will let Mr. Howe, who purchased Hurlburt's manuscript, give his version of this affair; simply reminding our readers that his book, "Mormonism Unveiled," was published in 1834, when the exact facts would be much fresher in the memory of the participants than in 1880. Speaking of the "Manuscript Found," he writes:

"It was inferred at once that some light might be shed upon this subject and the mystery revealed by applying to Patterson and Lambdin, in Pittsburg. But here again death had interposed a barrier. That establishment was dissolved and broken up many years since, and Lambdin died about eight years ago. Mr. Patterson says he has no recollection of any such manuscript being brought there for publication, neither would he have been likely to have seen it, as the business of printing was conducted wholly by Lambdin at that time. He says, however, that many manuscript books and pamphlets were brought to the office about that time, which remained upon the shelves for years without being printed or even examined."

Mark how strangely this statement disagrees with the assertions of the ladies of the Spaulding family with regard to Mr. Patterson's friendship and intimate acquaintance with Mr. Spaulding, and the latter's admiration of the "Manuscript Found."

Now notice the insincerity and actual dishonesty of the next passages, in view of the fact that Hurlburt had received the "Manuscript Found" from the Spaulding family, and according to his account had given the document that he had received to Howe, the publisher of the work from which we are quoting:

"Now as Spaulding's book can no where be found, or anything heard of it after being carried to this establishment, there is the strongest presumption that it remained there in seclusion till about the year 1823 or 1824, at which time Sidney Rigdon located himself in that city. We have been credibly informed that he was on terms of intimacy with Lambdin, being seen frequently at his shop."

Here is a desperate attempt to connect Rigdon with the affair. Lambdin was dead so he could not contradict any statement about his intimacy with Rigdon; but the whole hypothesis amounts to nothing in view of the positive statements of the Spaulding family that the "Manuscript Found" was in their undisturbed possession, hundreds of miles from Pittsburg, from 1814 to 1834. One thing, however, it shows that in those days Sidney Rigdon's life was too well known for Howe to write other than the truth regarding the time he first visited Pittsburg, for when Mrs. Dickenson wildly imagines and falsely asserts he was working in the office of Patterson and Lambdin, all trustworthy authorities, including his mother, assert that he was laboring upon his father's farm at St Clair, Alleghany Co., Pennsylvania, which he did not leave until he was in his twenty-sixth year, when he went to Ohio and afterwards to Pittsburg.

Possibly doubting the Spaulding story herself Mrs. Dickenson suggests another solution, yet still more ridiculous. She writes: "Smith, however, could easily have possessed himself of the manuscript if he had fancied it suitable to his purpose, for it is understood that he was a servant on the farm, or teamster for Mr. Sabine (Mrs. Spaulding's brother) in whose house the package of manuscript lay exposed in an unlocked trunk for several years."

Prodigious! Let us examine this wonderful suggestion. According to Mrs. McKinstry's affidavit the "Manuscript Found" was at Mr. Sabine's from 1816 to 1820. Joseph Smith was born in the latter part of December 1805, consequently he was not fifteen years old when the manuscript was removed from Mr. Sabine's. A boy of his age would make a rather youthful teamster or farm-hand. And then how preposterous the thought that an illiterate boy of eleven, twelve, or thirteen should conceive the idea of converting that old romance into something very like the Bible, and of founding a religious society on its principles! Then again calculate how much spare time a hired man or boy had on a farm in western New York fifty years ago; from sun up to sun down he was kept at work, often with chores to do after dark. How long would it take an ignorant boy under these circumstances, and lazy in the bargain, to transcribe a book that makes more than 600 pages of printed matter and contains, at a rough estimate, more than 300,000 words? Oh consistency! whither art thou fled?

But unfortunately for Mrs. Dickenson's very original theory, the testimony of all, friends and enemies alike, is positive that during this time Joseph was living with his father's family at Palmyra and other places. It is during this period of his life that the foes of divine revelation falsely charge him with confirmed idleness, vagabond habits, etc., and on this charge base their arguments that such a youth would never have been chosen by the Almighty as His servant. But should there be any doubt on this matter we extract a few lines from the already quoted affidavit of his sister, Mrs. Katherine Salisbury. When speaking of the publication of the Book of Mormon, she avers: "At the time the said book was published, I was seventeen years of age; that at the time of the publication of said book, my brother, Joseph Smith, Jr., lived in the family of my father, in the town of Manchester, Ontario county, New York, and that he had, all his life to this time made his home with the family." To which we may add during the latter years of this period occasionally hiring out for short intervals, but never at the early age and for the lengthened period necessary to give consistency to Mrs. Dickenson's suppositions. We shall pass by several other outrageous misstatements of this lady, and simply refer to one which purports to be from the veteran journalist, Thurlow Weed, simply to show how utterly unreliable many persons memories become where "Mormonism" is concerned.

Mr. Weed states that Joseph Smith called on him in 1825, desiring to get his manuscript printed, and spoke of finding the plates (Joseph did not obtain the plates until September, 1827, and the translation was not finished until June or July, 1829). That in a few days he brought Martin Harris (Harris was not associated with Joseph until after the plates were found). Seemed about thirty years of age (Joseph was not twenty until December 23rd of that year). Was about 5 feet 8 inches high (Joseph was fully 6 feet). Thus it appears in every detail Mr. Weed's memory was at fault; dates, age, hight, etc., are all wrong, very wrong, and his statement is untrustworthy from beginning to end.

In passing we draw attention to the difference between the size of the "Manuscript Found" and the Book of Mormon. The former, according to Mrs. McKinstry, was about one inch thick of *written*, not printed, matter. According to Hurlburt, the manuscript which he obtained from Mrs. Davison's chest, which she states was the "Manuscript Found," contained *about one quire of paper*. And this was the only manuscript book in the trunk. Mrs. Davison stated in her interview with Mr. Haven that the manuscript was about *one third* the size of the Book of Mormon; while Mr. Jackson said the romance was a very small work. All agree that it was much smaller than the Book of Mormon, while Hurlburt had evidently a motive in making out that it was less than it really was. He desired to make it appear that there must have been some other writings than the one he obtained. In any case it is a consistent question, who manufactured all the rest of the Book of Mormon?

CHAPTER V.
WHAT THE BOOK OF MORMON REALLY IS.

THE Book of Mormon is the record of God's dealings with the people of ancient America from the era of the building of the Tower of Babel to four hundred and twenty-one years after the birth of Christ. It is the stick of Ephraim spoken of by Ezekiel—the Bible of the western continent. Not that it supersedes, or in any way interferes with the Bible, any more than the history of Mexico supersedes or interferes with the history of Rome; but on the other hand, in many places it confirms Bible history, demonstrates Bible truths, sustains Bible doctrine, and fulfils Bible prophecy.

The Book of Mormon contains the history of two distinct races. The first came from the Tower of Babel and was destroyed a little less than six hundred years before Christ. The story of their national life is given very briefly, but sufficient is said to prove that they were one of the mightiest nations of antiquity, and in the days of their righteousness a people highly blessed of the Lord. Their fall and final destruction were the result of their gross wickedness and rejection of God's prophets. These people were called the Jaredites, their history in the Book of Mormon is contained in "the Book of Ether." Ether was one of their last prophets who wrote his account on twenty-four plates of gold. Moroni, the last prophet of the Nephites, abridged Ether's history and it is his abridgment that has been translated and published in this generation, and which forms a portion of the Book of Mormon.

The next race that inhabited this continent were of Israel-itish origin, the descendants of Joseph and Judah. The Nephites, the ruling branch, were principally the descendants of Manasseh. By divine guidance their first prophet and ruler, Lehi, was brought out of Jerusalem with a small company of his relatives and friends, eleven years before the Babylonian captivity (B. C. 600). They sailed from south-eastern Arabia across the Indian and Pacific oceans, and landed on the American shore not far from where the city of Valparaiso now stands. In the first year of the captivity another small colony was led out from Jerusalem, Mulek, one of the sons of King Zedekiah, being their nominal leader. This party landed in North America some distance north of the Isthmus of Darien, and soon after migrated into the northern portion of the southern continent, where for nearly four centuries they grew in numbers, but not in true civilization.

In the meantime the descendants of the colonists under Lehi had also grown numerous. Early in their history they had separated into two nationalities; the first, called Nephites, observing the laws of Moses, the teachings of the prophets, and developing in the decencies and comforts of civilized life; the others, called Lamanites (after the cruel, rebellious elder brother of Nephi), sank into barbarism and idolatry. These latter gradually crowded the Nephites northward until the latter reached the land occupied by the descendants of Mulek's colony, now called the people of Zarahemla, with whom they coalesced and formed one nation. From their national birth to B. C. 91, the Nephites had been ruled by kings, but at that time the form of government was changed and a republic founded. The nation was then ruled by judges elected by the people. This portion of the history of the Nephites is a very varied one. One third of their time they were engaged in actual war with the Lamanites, and at other times they were distracted with internal convulsions and rebellions. About A. D. 30, the republic was overthrown and the people split up into numerous independent tribes. At the crucifixion of the Savior this continent was the scene of terrible natural convulsions, which resulted in a great change in the face of nature and an immense loss of human life. Shortly after these days of terror the Redeemer appeared to the surviving remnants, taught them His gospel and organized His Church. A lengthened period of blessed peace followed in which all men served the Lord. Gradually, however, the old evils again crept in, many returned to the sins of their forefathers, the spirit of darkness and bloodshed again held sway, and finally the whole Nephite race was overpowered and destroyed (A. D. 384) by the other faction who had assumed the old name of Lamamites. The descendants of these Lamanites are found in the American Indians, not of the United States alone, but as the aborigines of the whole continent from Pat? , ..a to the Arctic ocean.

The records of this people, engraved on various plates were hid by the last of the Nephite prophets, Mormon, and his son Moroni. A portion thereof has, by God's grace, been restored to the knowledge of mankind in this age, and translated into many languages, that the truths contained therein, whether they be history, doctrine, or prophecy, may be known by all men.

CHAPTER VI.

UTTER DISAGREEMENT OF THE TWO HISTORIES.

IT is our purpose in this chapter to demonstrate, from the Book of Mormon itself, the absurdity of the "Spaulding Story," and the utter impossibility of the Prophet Joseph Smith ever having used Mr. Spaulding's reputed romance, the "Manuscript Found," as the groundwork for that divine record.

At different times since the publication of the Book of Mormon various writers have undertaken to explain the plot and contents of the "Manuscript Found," and to show how remarkable is the resemblance between it and the Book of Mormon.

We are told by one clerical author that when the Book of Mormon was read to Solomon Spaulding's widow, brother and six other persons, all well acquainted with Mr. Spaulding's writings, they immediately recognized in the Book of Mormon the same historical matter and names as composed the romance, although this reading took place some years after they had read the latter work. The writer further states that they affirmed that the Book of Mormon was with the exception of the religious matter, copied almost *word for word* from Spaulding's manuscript.

Another writer affirms that the romance of Spaulding was *similar in all its leading features* to the historical portions of the Book of Mormon. A third writer maintains that the historical part of the Book of Mormon was immediately recognized by all the older inhabitants of New Salem, Ohio, as *the identical work* of Mr. Spaulding, in which they had been so interested twenty years before.

Those who claim to have been acquainted with the writings of Mr. Spaulding, differ materially as to the incidents and plot of the "Manuscript Found." According to their widely different statements, his romance was based upon one of two theories. The first on the idea of the landing of a Roman colony on the Atlantic seaboard shortly before the Christian era. The second (now the most generally known and accepted) on the supposition that the present American Indians are the descendants of the ten tribes of Israel, who were led away captive out of their own land into Media, where historically the world loses sight of them, but where Mr. Spaulding's romance finds them and transports them to America. It is upon this idea of the transportation of this great and numerous people from the land of their captivity to the western world that this gentleman's novel is generally said to have been founded.

We will examine this statement first, and strive to discover how nearly it agrees with the historical narrative of the Book of Mormon, which we are told was immediately recognized as being *identical* and *copied almost word for word* from the pages of the "Manuscript Found."

In the first place, it is well to remark that the Book of Mormon makes but very few references to the ten tribes, and in those few, it directly, plainly and unequivocally states that the American Indians are not the descendants of the ten tribes, and further, that the ten tribes never were in America, or any part of it, during any portion of their existence as a nation.[*] On the other hand, the Book of Mormon as directly informs us from whom the aborigines, or natives, of this continent are descended. This being the case, how is it possible for the two works to be identical?

But admitting, for the sake of argument, that Joseph Smith might have changed the statement of the author of the "Manuscript Found" in this one particular, we will proceed to show that such a supposition is utterly impossible; for to have retained the unities of the work and the consistencies of the story (for the story of the Book of Mormon is consistent with itself), he must have altered not only the leading features but also the minor details of the whole historical narrative. He must have altered the place of departure, the circumstances of the journey, the route taken by the emigrants, the time of the emigration and every other particular connected with such a great movement. We must recollect that the Book of Mormon gives the account of a small colony (perhaps of about thirty

---

[*]——Our crucified Redeemer, in His teachings to the Nephites, thus refers to the ten tribes of the house of Israel:

"And behold this is the land of your inheritance, and the Father hath given it unto you. And not at any time hath the Father given me commandment that I should tell it unto your brethren at Jerusalem; neither at any time hath the Father given me commandment, that I should tell unto them concerning the other tribes of the house of Israel, whom the Father hath led away out of the land" (*III. Nephi, xv.* 13-15).

"That they" (the Jews) "may receive a knowledge of you by the Holy Ghost, and also of the other tribes whom they know not of" (*III. Nephi, xvi.* 4).

"The other tribes hath the Father separated from them" (*III. Nephi, xv.* 20).

"But now I go unto the Father, and also to show myself unto the lost tribes of Israel, for they are not lost unto the Father, for He knoweth whither He hath taken them" (*III. Nephi, xvii.* 4).

or forty souls) being led by the Lord from the city of Jerusalem through the wilderness south and east of that city, to the
borders of the Red Sea, thence for some distance in the same
direction near its coast, and then across the Arabian peninsula to
the sea eastward.   What insanity could have induced Mr.
Spaulding to propose such a route for the ten tribes?   For of
all out-of-the-way methods of reaching the American continent
from Media, this would be one of the most inaccessible, difficult, round-about and improbable, and would carry them along
the two sides of an acute angle by the time they reached the
shore where the ship was built.   It would almost certainly
have taken these tribes close to, if not through a portion of
their own ancient homes, where it is reasonable to suppose
nearly all would have desired to tarry, when we consider how
great was the love that ancient Israel bore for that rich land
given to them by divine power.

Mr. Spaulding, as a student of the Bible, would have made
no such blunder.   But even supposing that he was foolish
enough in his romance to transport the hosts of Israel from
the south-western borders of the Caspian Sea (where history
loses them) by the nearest route, most probably over the Arme-
nian mountains, across the Syrian desert, and by way of
Damascus through the lands of Gilead, Moab and Edom into
the wilderness of the Red Sea, where, we ask, is there an
account of such a journey in any portion of the Book of Mormon?   There is none, for the Book of Mormon opens with
the description of Lehi's departure from Jerusalem, with the
causes that led thereto, he having been a resident of that city
all his days, and never a captive in Media.   Therefore we are
justified in asking, at the very outset of this inquiry, where,
from the opening pages onward, is there any identity between
the two books?

Then, again, is it not obvious to every thinking person that
the moving of a nation, such as the ten tribes were, must have
had associated with it events and circumstances entirely inconsistent and at variance with the simple story of the journey of
Lehi and his family as given, frequently with minute detail,
in the Book of Mormon?   How numerous were the host of
the captive Israelites we have no means of definitely ascertain-

ing. We learn, however, that in one invasion alone, Shalmaneser, king of Assyria, carried off two hundred thousand captives from the kingdom of Israel. Even admitting that in their captivity these two hundred thousand did not increase in numbers, and entirely ignoring all the other thousands that were led away captives in other invasions, we should necessarily expect that Spaulding, in his account of the moving of this mass of humanity—men, women and children, with their flocks, herds and supplies—would write a narrative consistent with the subject and not one such as the Book of Mormon contains. But whether he did or did not, the Book of Mormon contains nothing whatever of the kind. In that work no vast armies are led out of Media by any route whatever to the American continent.

We have there an entirely different story, more dissimilar indeed from Spaulding's supposed narrative than the history of the deliverance of Israel out of Egypt, under Moses, is from the story of the departure from the old world, the voyage across the Atlantic and the landing on this continent of the Pilgrim Fathers, of revered memory. In the narrative that the Book of Mormon gives of the journeyings of Lehi and his little colony, all the incidents related are consistent with the idea of a small people and entirely inconsistent with that of a vast moving multitude.

For instance, let us take as an example, the story of Nephi breaking his bow by which the little caravan was placed in danger of starvation. If there had been a vast host, numbering nearly a quarter of a million souls, such an incident could have had no weight; for surely Mr. Spaulding never wrote that one hunter alone supplied such a multitude with all the necessary food, and it would be equally absurd to imagine that that gentleman would tell such an improbable story as that all the hunters broke all their bows at the same time. Again, the Book of Mormon tells us that Lehi and his companions depended on the chase for their entire food. Where, we would ask, in the midst of the Arabian desert, could game enough be found to supply the entire wants of the migrating ten tribes? And further, what would they do for water for such a company in the trackless Arabian desert without divine interposition and the manifestation of miraculous power? But the Book of Mormon hints at no such contingency.

Again, the story of the building of the ship by Nephi must have been entirely altered, for no one ship, though it had been twenty times as large as the *Great Eastern*, could have carried Mr. Spaulding's imaginary company and their effects across the wide waters of the Indian and Pacific oceans.

We must now draw attention to the time when the Book of Mormon states Lehi and his company were led out of Jerusalem. There is no ambiguity on this point. It is repeatedly stated that this event took place six hundred years before the advent of our Savior; that is, it was previous to the Babylonish captivity. The ten tribes were not lost sight of at that time; they were undoubtedly still in the land of their captivity, and if Mr. Spaulding was foolish enough in his romance to set a date to his exodus, he certainly would not have placed it during the lifetime of Jeremiah, the prophet, and of Nebuchadnezzar, king of Babylon; for not only would such a date have marred the consistency of the story, but it is also utterly impossible for us to conceive, as an historical probability, that the mighty king of Babylon would have permitted the ten tribes to escape from their captivity at that time, and above all things to have taken such a route as would have brought them near the borders of the Red Sea. If they escaped at all, it necessarily would have been to the uninhabited regions northward. From a political standpoint it would have been suicidal and utterly inconsistent with the polity of the king of Babylon to allow the captive Israelites to march forth in the supposed direction; for it would have placed them in immediate contact with the kingdom of Judah and enabled them to have formed an alliance with their former brethren antagonistic to his interest and policy.

To pursue the subject still further: when the colony reached the land of promise, which we call America, the incidents related in the Book of Mormon are entirely consistent with the story of the voyage and of the peopling of the land by a small colony and not by a vast host. If Joseph Smith, as some claim, had changed Mr. Spaulding's romance, he must have still continued to alter the narrative throughout the entire volume, for the story still maintains its consistency, and through it from beginning to end there runs a thread, possible only on the theory that it was a single family with their immediate connections through marriage that first founded the nations of the Nephites and Lamanites. The entire history hinges on the quarrels of the sons of Lehi and the results growing therefrom; for from the division of this family into two separate and distinct peoples grew all the wars, contentions, bloodshed, troubles and disasters that fill the pages of this sacred record; while on the other hand, the blessings flowing to both nations almost always resulted from the reconciliation of the two opposing peoples and the inauguration of a united and amicable policy beneficial alike to both. Had the American continent been peopled at the commencement by a vast host, the whole current of the story must have been vastly different, not only in the events that took place, but also in the motives that controlled the hearts of the actors who took part in those events, and in the traditions of the masses. In the case of the Nephites and Lamanites, these traditions had an overwhelming influence in the shaping of public affairs, which shape they never could have received by any set of traditions incidental to Mr. Spaulding's story.

What, too, shall we say of the Jaredites? From whence did Joseph Smith beg, borrow or steal their history? Did Mr. Spaulding bring his ten tribes from the tower of Babel, and give them an existence ages anterior to the lifetime of their great progenitor, Jacob? If not, will somebody inform us how this portion of the Book of Mormon was manufactured?

From the above it is evident that if Mr. Spaulding's story was what its friends claim, then it never could have formed the ground work of the Book of Mormon, for the whole historical narrative is different from beginning to end. And further, the story that certain old inhabitants of New Salem, who, it is said, recognized the Book of Mormon, either never made such a statement, or they let their imagination run away with their memory into the endorsement of a falsehood and an impossibility. Either way there is a lie; if they asserted that the Book of Mormon is identical with the "Spaulding story," then they are guilty of having violated the truth; if they did not make this statement, then the falsehood is with those who, in their hatred to modern revelation, have invented their testimony. The same statement applies to those who assert that the Book of Mormon was copied almost word for word from the "Manuscript Found." A book that is entirely dissimilar in its narrative cannot be exact in its wording. As well might we say, and be just as consistent and every way as truthful, that the history of England was copied from the adventures of Robinson Crusoe. So it is with the Book of Mormon and the Spaulding romance.

If then the resemblance is so small between the Book of Mormen and the "Manuscript Found," when we consider the ten tribe version of the latter work, where is it possible there can be the shadow of similarity when we examine the Roman colony theory? For instance:

Lehi left Jerusalem; Spaulding's heroes sailed from Rome.

Lehi started on his journey not knowing whither the Lord would lead him; the Romans were bound for Britain.

Lehi and his companions wandered for several years on land; the Roman party made the entire journey by water.

Lehi traveled by way of the Arabian peninsula and the Indian and Pacific oceans; Spaulding's imaginary characters sailed by way of the Mediterranean sea and the Atlantic ocean.

The travels of one party were considerably south of east; the voyage of the others west or north-west.

One party landed on the South Pacific shore; * the other on the North Atlantic.

---

*——Regarding the route taken by Lehi and his company, the Prophet Joseph Smith states:

"They traveled nearly a south, south-east direction until they came to the ninteenth degree of north latitude; then, nearly east to the sea of Arabia, then sailed in a south-east direction, and landed on the continent of South America, in Chili, thirty degrees south latitude."

Mormon's record was written in reformed Egyptian; the imaginary "Manuscript Found" in Latin.

Mormon's record was engraved on plates of metal; Spaulding's pretended manuscript was written on parchment.

The original of the Book of Mormon was hid in the hill Cumorah, state of New York; Mr. Spaulding's manuscript is claimed to have been discovered in a cave near Conneaut, state of Ohio.

The Book of Mormon gives an account of a religious people, God's dealings with whom is the central dominant idea; Spaulding's romance tells the story of an idolatrous people. Such is the positive statement of his widow and daughter.

There is another point worthy of our thought: If Joseph Smith did make use of the "Manuscript Found," it must have been for one of two reasons: Either because he was not able to write such a work himself, or that he might save himself trouble and labor. In the first place he could not have done this for the lack of ability; for any one who could have so adroitly altered a history of the ten tribes so that it now reads as a distinct, detailed and consistent history of a small company of the tribe of Joseph, most assuredly could have written such a history for himself if he had felt so disposed. Then again, he could not have done it to save himself work, for to so change a long history from one end to the other, until it contradicted all it had previously asserted. and became the harmonious history of another people, would save no man trouble. Then, again, in considering these points, we must remember what an "idle vagabond" Joseph was, according to some people's stories. What could have possibly possessed him to do such an enormous amount of copying, when, as illiterate as he was, such an operation would have been immensely hard work? Though it must be remembered all this time he was loafing round the street corners, telling fortunes and doing everything but honest toil—that is, if some people's tales are to be believed.

And, again, to show the weakness of our opponents' arguments, supposing for a moment that Joseph was an impostor, then he ran the risk of detection by copying another man's work, he ran that risk without a single motive, except it was the privilege of toiling for nothing, or the pleasure of being exposed, when by writing it himself he need have no risk at all.

CHAPTER VII.

JOSEPH SMITH'S EARLY LIFE.

THE supposed bad character of Joseph Smith when a youth has been made the text for many a tirade against the gospel that he, by God's grace, restored to the earth. How is it possible, it is asked, that we can believe that God would choose such an instrument for His work? We answer in the first place, God's ways are not as man's ways, and He has a perfect right to choose whomsoever He will. But further we assert, knowing we speak the truth, that the stories about Joseph Smith's bad character are false, and were never whispered until after God called him, and he had commenced the work that heaven assigned him. Until that time he and his parents with their entire family enjoyed a good reputation among their neighbors.

No sooner had Joseph borne his simple testimony of angelic visitations, than the evil one commenced to vilify his character, to destroy the effect of his testimony. Evil reports spread far and wide, growing as they went, as lies always do, until the days of D. P. Hurlburt, who, when going east to obtain the "Manuscript Found," made it his business to visit the neighborhood of Joseph's early home, and gather for publication all the floating scandal that had been in circulation from the beginning. He also procured an affidavit, or affidavits, which he asserted numbers of the old neighbors of the Smith family signed. Some of the persons whose names were attached to those papers have since repudiated all knowledge thereof, and make statements with regard to Joseph Smith's character entirely at :variance with the tenor of the affidavits. Others signed from hearsay and rumor and not from actual knowledge. Others are said to have been themselves men of such disreputable character that to be traduced by them was a compliment. The names of entire strangers were also added to swell the list. These fradulent and untruthful affidavits have been reprinted time and again, and others have followed in Hurlburt's footsteps, inventing other statements with regard to Joseph Smith, and attached the names of well-known residents of Palmyra, Manchester, etc., thereto without their knowledge and consent, and putting into their mouths statements entirely at variance with their sentiments and expressions. We regret to have to say that this dirty work has generally been done by professed ministers of the gospel.

The affidavits gathered by Hurlburt make the signers thereto complain that the Smith family, especially Joseph, was indolent, intemperate, untruthful, "entirely destitute of moral character and addicted to vicious habits." These charges are not only false, but they also manifest all the bitter hatred of religious bigotry and all the exaggeration of envy and revenge.

Joseph was undoubtedly not perfect—none of us are—but he was far superior in almost every respect to his neighbors and associates. In his own account of his youth, between the time of his first vision and the visit of the angel Moroni, he in the humility of his repentance fully confesses his youthful follies, and, as is natural with sensitive and consciencious natures, such as his, evidently applies the strongest language to his shortcomings, and exaggerates rather than extenuates his youthful misdeeds.

He writes:

"During the space of time which intervened between the time I had the vision and the year eighteen hundred and twenty-three (having been forbidden to join any of the religious sects of the day, and being of very tender years, and persecuted by those who ought to have been my friends, and to have treated me kindly, and if they supposed me to be deluded to have endeavored, in a proper and affectionate manner, to have reclaimed me), I was left to all kinds of temptations, and mingled with all kinds of society. I frequently fell into many foolish errors, and displayed the weakness of youth, and the corruption of human nature, which, I am sorry to say, led me into divers temptations, to the gratification of many appetites offensive in the sight of God. In consequence of these things I often felt condemned for my weakness and imperfections; when on the evening of the twenty-first of September, after I had retired to my bed for the night. I betook myself to prayer and supplication to Almighty God, for forgiveness of all my sins and follies, and also for a manifestation to me, that I might know of my state and standing before Him; for I had full confidence in obtaining a divine manifestation, as I had previously done."

The above is a simple, straightforward, artless statement of his condition, in which he seeks to hide nothing, but at the same time shows that the rebuffs he received, the persecutions he suffered from those who should have been his guides and friends had sufficient influence to cause him occasionally to give way to the weakness of youth incidental to association with the rough and unrestrained society he from his lowly position in life was naturally compelled to mingle with.

When comparing the before-mentioned vile charges with the testimony of those who knew the future Prophet's family best, we learn that instead of being indolent, the family were "good workers;" instead of being untruthful and vicious, they were honest, upright, religious and veracious, good neighbors, kind in sickness, but very poor, and with but little of the knowledge of this world. Their poverty, which some uncharitable souls have transformed into "shiftlessness," or lack of management, is one of the heaviest charges brought against them.

The charge of intemperance can be simmered down to the fact that on one or two occasions, in the harvest field, Joseph drank rather more cider than did him good. All the witnesses declare that "everybody drank in those days." It was before the age of temperance societies, and all classes of people considered it perfectly right to take a little strong drink occasionally. Drunkenness was the besetting sin of that era among the English race. Joseph was not a "teetotaler," because there were none. He was also very fond of wrestling, as many of his friends of later years know, and doubtless when stimulated with cider was on hand for a bout, or for any other athletic game or trial of strength that might be suggested. From this exuberance of animal spirits, the enemies of God's latter-day work have built up the story of Joseph's inebriety and vagabond character.

Again, he is charged with the grave offense of being a "money-digger." In one sense this is true. The whole country round about western New York was in those days affected with a mania to discover hidden treasures in the earth. Most marvelous stories are told of the interposition of unseen beings when some of these treasures were disturbed. The public mind was greatly troubled on this subject, and Joseph Smith was employed by a man at one time to dig for him in the hope of discovering some of these buried riches, or an ancient Spanish mine. Joseph worked for him as he would for any other man, or for the same man if he engaged him to plant potatoes or hoe corn. From this grew the story of Joseph being a money-digger. Even if he dug for treasure on his own responsibility, we do not know that there is anything degrading, dishonest or criminal in such an action.

The following is Joseph's own account of the manner in which he became saddled with the title of "Money-digger:"

"As my father's worldly circumstances were very limited, we were under the necessity of laboring with our hands, hiring by day's work and otherwise as we could get opportunity; sometimes we were at home and sometimes abroad, and by continued labor we were enabled to get a comfortable maintenance.

"In the year 1824, my father's family met with a great affliction, by the death of my eldest brother, Alvin. In the month of October, 1825, I hired with an old gentleman by the name of Josiah Stoal, who lived in Chenango county, State of New York. He had heard something of a silver mine having been opened by the Spaniards, in Harmony, Susquehanna county, state of Pennsylvania, and had, previous to my hiring with him, been digging, in order, if possible, to discover the mine. After I went to live with him he took me among the rest of his hands to dig for the silver mine, at which I continued to work for nearly a month without success in our undertaking, and finally I prevailed with the old gentleman to cease digging after it. Hence arose the very prevalent story of my having been a money-digger."

Somewhere about this time, or possibly rather later, Joseph worked for Mr. Joseph Knight, of Colesville, New York.

Of Joseph, Mr. Knight's son, Newel, writes in his private manuscript journal, as follows:

3

"The business my father was engaged in, often required him to have hired help, and among the many he, from time to time, employed was a young man by the name of Joseph Smith, Jun., to whom I was particularly attached. His noble deportment, his faithfulness, and his kind address could not fail to win the esteem of those who had the pleasure of his acquaintance. One thing I will mention which seemed to be a peculiar characteristic with him in all his boyish sports and amusements: I never knew anyone to gain advantage over him, and yet he was always kind and kept the good will of his playmates."

In March, 1881, two gentlemen, named Kelley, residing in Michigan, for their own satisfaction, visited the neighborhood where Joseph spent his youth, and questioned the older residents who were acquainted with the Smith family as to their knowledge of the character of Joseph, his parents and his brothers and sisters. Their interviews with numerous parties who claim to have known Joseph were afterwards published. Among those visited were the families, and sometimes the identical persons whose names had been appended, often without their knowledge, to former scurrilous affidavits regarding the reputation of the Smith family. In several cases these parties stated that they did not so much as know that any statement of theirs had ever been published; that they never uttered the sentiments or made the assertions attributed to them, and in some instances that they had been abused because they would not make the damaging statements regarding Joseph's character that those who visited them required. In many cases where they spoke disparagingly of the Prophet's family to the Messrs. Kelley, these gentlemen found that they spoke *from hearsay,* and *not from actual knowledge;* while those who knew Joseph best spoke of him the most highly. We here append a few extracts from these interviews, at the same time remarking (to put the feeling in the mildest language), that some of these gentlemen were no friends of the Smith family.

"What did you know about the Smiths, Mr. Gilbert?"

"I knew nothing myself; have seen Joseph Smith a few times, but not acquainted with him. Saw Hyrum quite often. I am the party that set the type from the original manuscript for the Book of Mormon. They translated it in a cave. I would know that manuscript to-day if I should see it. The most of it was in Oliver Cowdery's handwriting. Some in Joseph's wife's; a small part though. Hyrum Smith always brought the manuscript to the office; he would have it under his coat, and all buttoned up as carefully as though it was so much gold. He said at the time that it was translated from plates by the power of God, and they were very particular about it. We had a great deal of trouble with it. It was not punctuated at all. They did not know anything about punctuation, and we had to do that ourselves."

"Well; did you change any part of it when you were setting the type?"

"No, sir; we never changed it at all."

"Why did you not change it and correct it?

"Because they would not allow us to; they were very particular about that. We never changed it in the least. Oh, well; there might have been one or two words that I changed the spelling of; I believe I did change the spelling of one, and perhaps two, but no more."

"Did you set all the type, or did some one help you?"

"I did the whole of it myself, and helped to read the proof, too; there was no one who worked at that but myself. Did you ever see one of the first copies? I have one here that was never bound. Mr. Grandin, the printer, gave it to me. If you ever saw a Book of Mormon you will see that they changed it afterwards."

"They did! Well, let us see your copy; that is a good point. How is it changed now?"

"I will show you (bringing out his copy). Here on the title page it says (reading), 'Joseph Smith, Jr., author and proprietor.' Afterwards, in getting out other editions they left that out, and only claimed that Joseph Smith translated it."

"Well, did they claim anything else than that he was the translator when they brought the manuscript to you?"

"Oh, no; they claimed that he was translating by means of some instruments he got at the same time he did the plates, and that the Lord helped him."

The Messrs. Kelley also called upon Dr. John Stafford, at Rochester, N. Y. He is now a retired physician, being too aged and infirm to practice. Answering a question as to the character of Joseph Smith, he said:

"He was a real clever, jovial boy. What Tucker said about them" (the Smith family) "was false, absolutely. My father, William Stafford, was never connected with them in any way. The Smiths, with others, were digging for money before Joe got the plates. My father had a stone, which some thought they could look through, and old Mrs. Smith came there for it

one day, but never got it.   Saw them digging one time for
money; (this was three or four years before the Book of Mormon was found) the Smiths and others.   The old man and
Hyrum were there, I think. but Joseph was not there.   The
neighbors used to claim Sally Chase could look at a stone she
had, and see money.   Willard Chase used to dig when she
found where the money was.   Don't know as anybody ever
found any money.''

"What was the character of Smith, as to his drinking?''

"It was common then for everybody to drink, and to have
drink in the field; one time Joe, while working for some one
after he was married, drank too much boiled cider.   He came
in with his shirt torn; his wife felt bad about it, and when
they went home, she put her shawl on him.''

"Had he been fighting and drunk?''

"No; he had been scuffling with some of the boys.   Never
saw him fight;   have known him to scuffle;   would do a fair
day's work if hired out to a man; but were poor managers,''
(the Smiths.)

"What about that black sheep your father let them have?''

"I have heard that story, but don't think my father was
there at the time they say Smith got the sheep.   I don't
know anything about it.''   .

"You were living at home at the time, and it seems you
ought to know if they got a sheep, or stole one, from your
father?''

"They never stole one, I am sure; they may have got one
sometime.''

"Well, doctor, you know pretty well whether that story is
true or not, that Tucker tells.   What do you think of it?''

"I don't think it is true.   I would have heard more about
it, that is true.   I lived a mile from Smith's; am seventy-six
years old.   They were peaceable among themselves.   The old
woman had a great deal of faith that their children were going
to do something great.   Joe was quite illiterate.   After they
began to have school at their house, he improved greatly.''

"Did they have school in their own house?''

"Yes, sir; they had school in their house, and studied the
Bible.''

"Who was their teacher?''

"They did not have any teacher; they taught themselves.''
   *   *   *   *   *   *   *

"If young Smith was illiterate as you say, doctor, how do
you account for the Book of Mormon?'

"Well, I can't; except that Sidney Rigdon was connected
with them.''

"What makes you think he was connected with them?''

"Because I can't account for the Book of Mormon any
other way.''

"Was Rigdon ever around there before the Book of Mormon was published?"

"No; not as we could ever find out. Sidney Rigdon was never there, that Hurlburt, or Howe, or Tucker could find out."

"Well; you have been looking out for the facts a long time have you not, doctor?"

"Yes; I have been thinking and hearing about it for the last fifty years, and lived right among all their old neighbors there most of the time."

"And no one has ever been able to trace the acquaintance of Rigdon and Smith, until after the Book of Mormon was published, and Rigdon proselyted by Pratt, in Ohio?"

"Not that I know of."

   *   *   *   *   *   *   *

"Were you acquainted with them" (the Smiths) "Mr. Saunders?"

"Yes, sir, I knew all of the Smith family well; there were six boys: Alvin, Hyrum, Joseph, Harrison, William and Carlos, and there were two girls; the old man was a cooper; they have all worked for me many a day; they were very good people. Young Joe (as we called him then), has worked for me, and he was a good worker; they all were. I did not consider them good managers about business, but they were poor people; the old man had a large family."

"In what respect did they differ from other people, if at all?"

"I never noticed that they were different from other neighbors; they were the best family in the neighborhood in case of sickness; one was at my house nearly all the time when my father died; I always thought them honest; they were owing me some money when they left here; that is, the old man and Hyrum did, and Martin Harris. One of them came back in about a year and paid me."

"How were they as to habits of drinking and getting drunk?"

"Everybody drank a little in those days, and the Smiths with the rest; they never got drunk to my knowledge."

   *   *   *   *   *   *   *

"How well did you know young Joseph Smith?"

"Oh! just as well as one could very well; he has worked for me many a time, and been about my place a great deal. He stopped with me many a time, when through here, after they went west to Kirtland; he was always a gentleman when about my place."

"What did you know about his finding that book, or the plates in the hill over here?"

"He always claimed that he saw the angel and received the book; but I don't know anything about it. Have seen it, but never read it as I know of; didn't care anything about it."

"Well; you seem to differ a little from a good many of the stories told about these people."

"I have told you just what I know about them, and you will have to go somewhere else for a different story."

*   *   *   *   *   *   *

"To our inquiries if he, Mr. Thos. H. Taylor, was acquainted with the Smiths, and the early settlers throughout that part, sometimes called Mormons, he said:"

"Yes; I knew them very well; they were very nice men, too; the only trouble was they were ahead of the people; and the people, as in every such case, turned out to abuse them, because they had the manhood to stand for their own convictions. I have seen such work all through life, and when I was working with John Brown for the freedom of my fellow-man, I often got in tight places; and if it had not been for Gerritt Smith, Wendell Phillips and some others, who gave me their influence and money, I don't know how I would ever have got through."

"What did the Smiths do that the people abused them so?"

"They did not do anything. Why! these rascals at one time took Joseph Smith and ducked him in the pond that you see over there, just because he preached what he believed, and for nothing else. And if Jesus Christ had been there, they would have done the same to Him. Now I don't believe like he did; but every man has a right to his religious opinions, and to advocate his views, too; if people don't like it, let them come out and meet him on the stand, and show his error. Smith was always ready to exchange views with the best men they had."

"Why didn't they like Smith?"

"To tell the truth, there was something about him they could not understand; some way he knew more than they did, and it made them mad."

"But a good many tell terrible stories, about them being low people, rogues and liars, and such things. How is that?"

"Oh! they are a set of d—d liars. I have had a home here, and been here, except when on business, all my life— ever since I came to this country, and I know these fellows, they make these lies on Smith, because they love a lie better than the truth. I can take you to a great many old settlers here who will substantiate what I say, and if you want to go, just come around to my place across the street here, and I'll go with you."

"Well, that is very kind, Mr. Taylor, and fair; and if we have time we will call around and give you the chance; but we are first going to see these fellows who, so rumor says, know so much against them."

"All right; but you will find they don't know anything against those men when you put them down to it; they could never sustain anything against Smith."

"Do you think Smith ever got any plates out of the hill he claimed to?"

"Yes; I rather think he did. Why not he find something as well as anybody else? Right over here, in Illinois and Ohio, in mounds there, they have discovered copper plates since, with hieroglyphics all over them; and quite a number of the old settlers around here testified that Smith showed the plates to them—they were good, honest men, and what is the sense in saying they lied? Now, I never saw the Book of Mormon—don't know anything about it, nor care; and don't know as it was ever translated from the plates. You have heard about the Spaulding romance; and some claim that it is nothing but the books of the Bible that were rejected by the compilers of the Bible; but all this don't prove that Smith never got any plates."

We close this chapter with an extract from the writings of Elder Oliver Cowdery, published in a very early day of the Church's history:

"But in consequence of certain false and slanderous reports which have been circulated, justice would require me to say something upon the private life of one whose character has been so shamefully traduced. By some he is said to have been a lazy, idle, vicious, profligate fellow. These I am prepared to contradict, and that, too, by the testimony of *many* persons with whom I have been intimately acquainted, and know to be individuals of the strictest veracity and unquestionable integrity. All these strictly and virtually agree in saying, that he was an honest, upright, virtuous and faithfully industrious young man. And those who say to the contrary can be influenced by no other motive than to destroy the reputation of one who never injured any man in either property or person."

CHAPTER VIII.

JOSEPH'S ACCOUNT OF THE DISCOVERY OF THE PLATES.

WE will now give the Prophet Joseph's own narrative of the finding of the plates from which he, by divine aid, translated the Book of Mormon, with the causes that led thereto. It is a simple, unvarnished statement of facts that bears on its face the evidence of its truth.

On the evening of September 21st, 1823, Joseph went to bed with a strong feeling of regret for his youthful follies, and with a determination to seek the Lord for forgiveness and for a manifestation of his standing before heaven. With this desire, in strong faith, he betook himself to prayer and supplication. He then says:

"While I was thus in the act of calling upon God, I discovered a light appearing in the room, which continued to increase until the room was lighter than at noonday, when immediately a personage appeared at my bedside, standing in the air, for his feet did not touch the floor. He had on a loose robe of most exquisite whiteness. It was a whiteness beyond anything earthly I had ever seen; nor do I believe that any earthly thing could be made to appear so exceedingly white and brilliant; his hands were naked, and his arms also, a little above the wrist; so, also, were his feet naked, as were his legs, a little above the ankles. His head and neck were also bare. I could discover that he had no other clothing on but this robe, as it was open, so that I could see into his bosom.

"Not only was his robe exceedingly white, but his whole person was glorious beyond description, and his countenance truly like lightning. The room was exceedingly light, but not so very bright as immediately around his person. When I first looked upon him I was afraid, but the fear soon left me. He called me by name and said unto me that he was a messenger sent from the presence of God to me, and that his name was Moroni. That God had a work for me to do, and that my name should be had for good and evil among all nations, kindreds, and tongues; or that it should be both good and evil spoken of among all people. He said there was a book deposited, written upon gold plates, giving an account of the former inhabitants of this continent, and the source from whence they sprang. He also said that the fulness of the everlasting gospel was contained in it, as delivered by the Savior to the ancient inhabitants. Also, that there were two stones in silver bows (and these stones, fastened to a breastplate, constituted what is called the Urim and Thummim) deposited with the plates, and the possession and use of these stones were what constituted Seers in ancient or former times, and that God had prepared them for the purpose of translating the book.

"Again, he told me that when I got those plates of which he had spoken (for the time that they should be obtained was not yet fulfilled) I should not show them to any person, neither the breastplate with the Urim and Thummim, only to those to whom I should be commanded to show them; if I did, I should be destroyed. While he was conversing with me about the plates, the vision was opened to my mind that I could see the place where the plates were deposited, and that so clearly and distinctly, that I knew the place again when I visited it.

"After this communication, I saw the light in the room begin to gather immediately around the person of him who had been speaking to me, and it continued to do so, until the room was again left dark, except just around him, when instantly I saw, as it were, a conduit open right up into heaven, and he ascended up till he entirely disappeared, and the room was left as it had been before this heavenly light had made its appearance.

"I lay musing on the singularity of the scene, and marveling greatly at what had been told me by this extraordinary messenger, when, in the midst of my meditation, I suddenly discovered that my room was again beginning to get lighted, and in an instant, as it were, the same heavenly messenger was again by my bedside. He commenced, and again related the very same things which he had done at his first visit, without the least variation, which having done, he informed me of great judgments which were coming upon the earth, with great desolations by famine, sword, and pestilence, and that these grievous judgments would come on the earth in this generation. Having related these things, he again ascended as he had done before.

"By this time, so deep were the impressions made on my mind, that sleep had fled from my eyes, and I lay overwhelmed in astonishment at what I had both seen and heard; but what was my surprise when again I beheld the same messenger at my bedside, and heard him rehearse or repeat over again to me the same things as before, and added a caution to me, telling me that Satan would try to tempt me (in consequence of the indigent circumstances of my father's family) to get the plates for the purpose of getting rich. This he forbid me, saying that I must have no other object in view in getting the plates but to glorify God, and must not be influenced by any other motive but that of building His kingdom, otherwise I could not get them. After this third visit, he again ascended up into heaven as before, and I was again left to ponder on the strangeness of what I had just experienced, when almost immediately after the heavenly messenger had ascended from me the third time, the cock crew, and I found that day was approaching, so that our interviews must have occupied the whole of that night. I shortly after arose from my bed, and, as usual, went to the necessary labors of the day, but, in attempting to labor as at other times, I found my strength so exhausted as rendered me entirely unable. My father, who was laboring along with me, discovered something to be wrong with me, and told me to go home. I started with the intention of going to the house, but, in attempting to cross the fence out of the field where we were, my strength entirely failed me, and I fell helpless on the ground, and for a time was quite unconscious of anything. The first thing that I can recollect, was a voice speaking unto me calling me by name; I looked up and beheld the same messenger standing over my head, surrounded by light, as before. He then again related unto me all that he had related to me the previous night, and commanded me to go to my father, and tell him of the vision and commandments which I had received.

"I obeyed, I returned back to my father in the field and rehearsed the whole matter to him. He replied to me that it was of God, and to go and do as commanded by the messenger. I left the field and went to the place where the messenger had told me the plates were deposited, and owing to the distinctness of the vision which I had had concerning it, I knew the place the instant that I arrived there. Convenient to the village of Manchester, Ontario county, New York, stands a hill of considerable size, and the most elevated of any in the neighborhood. On the west side of this hill, not far from the top, under a stone of considerable size, lay the plates, deposited in a stone box; this stone was thick and rounding in the middle on the upper side, and thinner towards the edges, so that the middle part of it was visible above the ground, but the edge all round was covered with earth. Having removed the earth and obtained a lever which I got fixed under the edge of the stone, and with a little exertion raised it up; I looked in, and there indeed did I behold the plates, the Urim and Thummim, and the breastplate as stated by the messenger. The box in which they lay was formed by laying stones together in some kind of cement. In the bottom of the box were laid two stones crossways of the box, and on these stones lay the plates and the other things with them. I made an attempt to take them out, but was forbidden by the messenger, and was again informed that the time for bringing them forth had not yet arrived, neither would arrive until four years from that time; but he told me that I should come to that place precisely in one year from that time, and that he would there meet with me, and that I should continue to do so until the time should come for obtaining the plates.

"Accordingly as I had been commanded, I went at the end of each year, and at each time I found the same messenger there, and received instruction and intelligence from him at each of our interviews, respecting what the Lord was going to do, and how and in what manner His kingdom was to be conducted in the last days.

"At length the time arrived for obtaining the plates, the Urim and Thummim, and the breastplate. On the 22nd day of September, 1827, having gone, as usual, at the end of another year, to the place where they were deposited, the same heavenly messenger delivered them up to me with this charge, that I should be responsible for them; that if I should let them go carelessly or through any neglect of mine, I should be cut off; but that if I would use all my endeavors to preserve them, until he, the messenger, should call for them, they should be protected.

"I soon found out the reason why I had received such strict charges to keep them safe, and why it was the messenger had said, that when I had done what was required at my hand, he would call for them; for no sooner was it known that I had them, than the most strenuous exertions were used to get them from me; every stratagem that could be invented was resorted to for that purpose; the persecution became more bitter and severe than before, and multitudes were on the alert continually to get them from me if possible; but, by the wisdom of God, they remained safe in my hands, until I had accomplished by them what was required at my hand; when according to arrangements, the messenger called for them, I delivered them up to him, and he has them in his charge until this day, being the 2nd day of May, 1838.

"The excitement, however, still continued, and rumor, with her thousand tongues, was all the time employed in circulating tales about my father's family, and about myself. If I were to relate a thousandth part of them, it would fill up volumes. The persecution, however, became so intolerable that I was under the necessity of leaving Manchester, and going with

my wife to Susquehanna county, in the state of Pennsylvania.
While preparing to start (being very poor, and the persecution
so heavy upon us, that there was no probability that we would
ever be otherwise), in the midst of our afflictions we found a
friend in a gentleman, by the name of Martin Harris, who
came to us and gave me fifty dollars to assist us in our afflictions.   Mr. Harris was a resident of Palmyra township,
Wayne county, in the state of New York, and a farmer of
respectability.   By this timely aid was I enabled to reach the
place of my destination in Pennsylvania, and immediately after
my arrival there, I commenced copying the characters of the
plates.   I copied a considerable number of them, and by
means of the Urim and Thummim I translated some of them,
which I did between the time I arrived at the house of my
wife's father in the month of December, and the February
following.

"Some time in this month of February, the afore-mentioned
Mr. Martin Harris came to our place, got the characters which
I had drawn off the plates, and started with them to the city
of New York.   For what took place relative to him and the
characters, I refer to his own account of the circumstances
as he related them to me after his return, which was as
follows :

" 'I went to the city of New York, and presented the characters which had been translated, with the translation thereof,
to Professor Anthon, a gentleman celebrated for his literary
attainments.   Professor Anthon stated that the translation
was correct, more so than any he had before seen translated
from the Egyptian.   I then showed him those which were not
yet translated, and he said that they were Egyptian, Chaldaic,
Assyraic, and Arabic, and he said that they were the true
characters.   He gave me a certificate, certifying to the people
of Palmyra that they were true characters, and that the translation of such of them as had been translated was also correct.
I took the certificate and put it into my pocket, and was just
leaving the house, when Mr. Anthon called me back and
asked me how the young man found out that there were gold
plates in the place where he found them.   I answered that an
angel of God had revealed it unto him.

" 'He then said unto me, 'Let me see that certificate.'   I
accordingly took it out of my pocket and gave it to him, when
he took it and tore it to pieces, saying that there was no such
thing now as ministering of angels, and that if I would bring
the plates to him, he would translate them.   I informed him
that part of the plates were sealed, and that I was forbidden
to bring them ; he replied, 'I cannot read a sealed book.'   I
left him and went to Dr. Mitchell, who sanctioned what Pro-

fessor Anthon had said respecting both the characters and the translation.'

"On the 15th [5th] day of April, 1829, Oliver Cowdery came to my house, until then I had never seen him. He stated to me that having been teaching school in the neighborhood where my father resided, and my father being one of those who sent to the school, he went to board for a season at his house, and while there, the family related to him the circumstance of my having the plates, and accordingly he had come to make inquiries of me.

"Two days after the arrival of Mr. Cowdery (being the 17th [7th] of April), I commenced to translate the Book of Mormon, and he commenced to write for me."

The foregoing is the Prophet Joseph's own account of the discovery of the plates, with some details as to the manner of their translation. We will now insert the testimony of the witnesses, who, by divine permission, saw, handled and examined these sacred records, and afterwards draw attention to the value of this testimony, more especially to that of the three witnesses, whose lives for so long a period were estranged from the Church and people to whom their words are of most value.

THE TESTIMONY OF THREE WITNESSES.

Be it known unto all nations, kindreds, tongues and people unto whom this work shall come, that we, through the grace of God the Father, and our Lord Jesus Christ, have seen the plates which contain this record, which is a record of the people of Nephi, and also of the Lamanites, their brethren, and also of the people of Jared, who came from the tower of which hath been spoken; and we also know that they have been translated by the gift and power of God, for His voice hath declared it unto us; wherefore we know of a surety that the work is true. And we also testify that we have seen the engravings which are upon the plates; and they have been shown unto us by the power of God, and not of man. And we declare with words of soberness, that an angel of God came down from heaven, and He brought and laid before our eyes, that we beheld and saw the plates, and the engravings thereon; and we know that it is by the grace of God the Father, and our Lord Jesus Christ, that we beheld and bear record that these things are true; and it is marvelous in our eyes, nevertheless the voice of the Lord commanded us that we should bear record of it; wherefore, to be obedient unto the commandments of God, we bear testimony of these things. And we know that if we are faithful in Christ, we shall rid our garments of the blood of all men, and be found spotless before the judgment-seat of Christ, and shall dwell with Him eternally in the heavens. And the honor be to the Father, and to the Son, and to the Holy Ghost, which is one God. Amen.

> OLIVER COWDERY,
> DAVID WHITMER,
> MARTIN HARRIS.

AND ALSO THE TESTIMONY OF EIGHT WITNESSES.

Be it known unto all nations, kindreds, tongues and people unto whom this work shall come, that Joseph Smith, Jun., the translator of this work, has shewn unto us the plates of which hath been spoken, which have the appearance of gold; and as many of the leaves as the said Smith has translated, we did handle with our hands; and we also saw the engravings thereon, all of which has the appearance of ancient work, and of curious workmanship. And this we bear record with words of soberness, that the said Smith has shewn unto us, for we have seen and hefted, and know of a surety that the said Smith has got the plates of which we have spoken. And we give our names unto the world, to witness unto the world that which we have seen; and we lie not, God bearing witness of it.

> CHRISTIAN WHITMER,   HIRAM PAGE,
> JACOB WHITMER,   JOSEPH SMITH, Sen.
> PETER WHITMER, Jun.   HYRUM SMITH,
> JOHN WHITMER,   SAMUEL H. SMITH.

CHAPTER IX.
TIME OCCUPIED IN TRANSLATING THE BOOK OF MORMON.

OBJECTION has been made to the divinity of the Book of Mormon on the ground that the account given in the publications of the Church, of the time occupied in the work of translation is far too short for the accomplishment of such a labor, and consequently it must have been copied or transcribed from some work written in the English language, most probably from Spaulding's "Manuscript Found." But at the outset it must be recollected that the translation was accomplished by no common method, by no ordinary means. It was done by divine aid. There were no delays over obscure passages, no difficulties over the choice of words, no stoppages from the ignorance of the translator; no time was wasted in investigation or argument over the value, intent or meaning of certain characters, and there were no references to authorities. These difficulties to human work were removed. All was as simple as when a clerk writes from dictation. The translation of the characters appeared on the Urim and Thummim, sentence by sentence, and as soon as one was correctly transcribed the next would appear. So the enquiry narrows down to the consideration of this simple question, how much could Oliver Cowdery write in a day? How many of the printed pages of the Book of Mormon could an ordinary clerk transcribe from dictation in a day? When that is determined, divide the total number of pages in the Book of Mormon by that number and you have the answer in days.

It now becomes important to discover when the translation was commenced and when it was finished. This cannot be determined to a day, but enough is known for our purpose.

When Oliver first visited Joseph some little had been translated, exactly how much is not known. The next question is:

When did that visit occur? We will let Oliver answer. He writes (*Times and Seasons Vol. I., page* 201): "Near the time of the setting of the sun, Sabbath evening, April 5th, 1829, my natural eyes, for the first time, beheld this brother. He then resided in Harmony, Susquehanna county, Pennsylvania. On Monday, the 6th, I assisted him in arranging some business of a temporal nature, and on Tuesday, the 7th, commenced to write the Book of Mormon."

In the history of Joseph Smith, we read: "During the month of April I continued to translate and he (Oliver) to write with little cessation, during which time we received several revelations." And again: "We still continued the work of translation, when, in the ensuing month (May 1829) we, on a certain day went into the woods to pray." Oliver also states: "These were days never to be forgotten—to sit under the sound of a voice dictated by the inspiration of heaven awakened the utmost gratitude of this bosom! Day after day I continued, uninterrupted, to write from his mouth, as he translated with the Urim and Thummim, or, as the Nephites would have said, 'Interpreters,' the history or record called the Book of Mormon."

Thus we see these two young men bent the whole energy of their souls towards the accomplishment of this most important work. They united their youthful zeal "day after day, uninterrupted" and "with little cessation" to the labor of translation. It requires very little imagination to understand how diligently and earnestly they toiled, how they permitted nothing to interfere with their labor of love, how they devoted every hour, until fatigue overcame them, to the divinely imposed task (and young and vigorous as they were it was not a little that would tire them out), while curiosity and other far worthier feelings would give zest and inspiration to their labors; as they progressed we can well imagine how their interest in the narrative increased until they could scarcely tear themselves away from their inspired labors even when their minds and bodies called for food and rest. The enthusiasm with which Oliver speaks of those days shows plainly that this was the case, and we cannot reasonably think that Joseph was any less interested than he.

Now let us examine when these two brethren commenced their marvelous work. Two series of dates have been given. Oliver's given above, and another in the history of Joseph Smith, which gives the dates as the 15th and 17th of April, or ten days later. Oliver's has this evidence of its correctness, that, as he states, the 5th, 6th and 7th of April, 1829, fell on Sunday, Monday and Tuesday, which, of course, those ten days later would not. Again, the event being of more importance in his life than in Joseph's, he was more likely to recollect the details, besides, being a better scholar and penman, it is more probable that if any record of the circumstance was made at that time he made it. But really there is no discrepancy. The dates 15th and 17th in the Pearl of Great Price, in Joseph's history, etc., are unfortunately typographical errors, or mistakes in printing. In the original manuscript in the Historian's Office the dates are the same as those of Oliver Cowdery—the 5th and 7th. But the mistake having once been printed it has been copied out of one journal or book into another until nearly all our works have perpetuated the blunder. Of course it is impossible to tell now whether the mistake was first made by a copyist in the Historian's Office or by a compositor at the printer's.

From Joseph's and Oliver's narrative we learn how far they had progressed in the work of translation at the time of the visit of the angel, John the Baptist, and their baptism. This took place on May 15th of the same year. It was because they found in the teachings of the risen Redeemer to the Nephites certain instructions regarding baptism that they were led to enquire of the Lord regarding this ordinance, and their inquiry led to the angel's visit. Where are these teachings found? In the third book of Nephi; some, probably the very ones that so deeply impressed the minds of these young men, on page five hundred and three of the Book of Mormon (latest edition). Then it is evident that between April 7th and May 15th they had translated as much as makes five hundred and three pages of the printed Book of Mormon. How much is this a day? Between these two dates, including April 7th but not May 15th, there are thirty-eight days, which would make about thirteen pages a day, if we

3*

allow nothing for what was previously transcribed. A swift writer copying from dictation could write four such pages in an hour, as we have demonstrated experimentally, an ordinary writer about three. But allowing that Oliver Cowdery might be a very slow writer, and that he only copied at the rate of a page in half an hour, even then he would only have had to work six and one half hours each day to accomplish the task; and if they rested entirely on Sundays about one hour more. So we see, making no allowance for the work already done, allowing Oliver Cowdery to be a slow penman for his profession—a schoolmaster—and admitting that they ceased from their labor on the Sabbath, still it was only necessary for them to do a short day's work, especially for two young men in the prime and vigor of life; and yet allow ample time for the reception of revelations (which were given through the Urim and Thummim) and the performance of other duties that possibly occasionally called for their attention.

To show how easy such an effort would be we will state that President George Q. Cannon has informed us that when he translated the Book of Mormon into the language of the Sandwich Islanders, he frequently translated as many as eight or ten pages a day. This was far heavier work to do alone, and without the assistance of the Urim and Thummim, than it was for Joseph and Oliver together to translate from twelve to fifteen pages with the all-important assistance of the "Interpreters."

After the date of their baptism, the brethren appear to have worked more leisurely. Early in June they moved to Mr. Peter Whitmer's, at Fayette, Seneca county, New York, who had kindly offered them a house. Here the work was continued, John Whitmer, one of the sons, assisting them very much by writing. Joseph states: "Meanwhile our translation was drawing to a close, we went to Palmyra, Wayne county, New York, secured the copyright and agreed with Mr. Egbert Grandin to print five thousand copies for the sum of three thousand dollars." The copyright was secured on June 11th, so it appears that between May 15th and the last-named date, or twenty-six days, they had not quite translated one hundred and twenty pages—not five pages a day—or they would have finished their work. The exact date the translation was entirely completed is not known, at least we have not been able to discover it.

Thus we see between the dates given, Joseph and Oliver had ample time to do the work claimed by and for them, the objection falls to the ground, and the truth is again vindicated.

<hr/>

CHAPTER X.
THE THREE WITNESSES.

IN the investigation of the genuineness of the Book of Mormon we must consider the nature of the direct evidence that we have with regard to its origin. And in this respect the testimony is strong, clear, complete and unimpeachable. The existence of the plates is testified to in a most solemn and sacred manner by eleven witnesses in addition to Joseph Smith. Eight of these witnesses actually handled, lifted, and carefully examined the plates, satisfying themselves in a manner beyond all dispute that the plates were real and tangible. It is altogether unlikely that Joseph Smith could have imposed upon these eight witnesses by giving into their hands something different from metallic plates. So, at any rate, we have the evidence of eight men that they handled certain plates and that they had the appearance of very ancient workmanship. If these plates were not the plates from which the Book of Mormon was translated, what were they? where did Joseph Smith get them? and what did he do with them? are all pertinent inquiries. That he had plates in his possession of the kind and description from which he states he translated the Book of Mormon is strong *prima facie* evidence in favor of his story. And the fact that he only showed them to certain few individuals is another evidence of the truthfulness of his statement; for if he, as is claimed, was an ignorant impostor, he would have naturally argued that to the more persons he showed his spurious plates, the wider would grow his influence and the greater would be the number of believers in his story. To keep the plates hidden from the multitude would naturally appear in the average mind to be the surest way of retarding his success and blocking his own progress; and assuredly if Joseph Smith had the cunning and dexterity to invent the story of the discovery of the plates and to manufacture a set of plates to agree with the story, he would have had cunning enough to present them to the public, surrounded by so much mystery and glamour that while they saw them they would not be able to examine them critically.

But we have greater and stronger evidence than that of these eight witnes-es. We have the testimony of three other men that the plates from which the Book of Mormon was translated were shown to them by an angel of the Lord, and not the plates only, but the engravings upon them; and still further they declare that they know that these plates were translated by the gift and power of God, for His voice had declared it unto them. Here, then, we not only have testimony of the existence of the plates, but also to their genuineness and to the truthfulness of the translation, which translation we have in the shape of the Book of Mormon. And it must be remembered that not one of these three witnesses has ever denied his testimony, or contradicted it in the least particular, but under all circumstances and upon every occasion all have in the strongest and most decided language declared that their testimony was true. Again, there is one very note-worthy fact with regard to these three men. They were all severed from the communion of the Church during the life-time of the Prophet Joseph. If Joseph Smith had been an impostor, he was in the power of each of these "three witnesses;" for any one of them, whenever he pleased, could have exposed the conspiracy, if conspiracy there had been, and shown to the world how the testimony had been manufactured; but none of them have ever done so. Although, at certain periods of their lives, they smarted under the denunciations and reproofs they received from the Prophet and entertained towards him the most bitter feelings for the course he took towards them, going so far as to denounce him as a fallen prophet, yet with all their acrimony and hatred they never once deviated from the testimony that is printed above their names at the commencement of the Book of Mormon. We appeal to all reasonable minds, and ask if it is possible to suppose that, if the Book of Mormon were a fraud, Joseph Smith would have dared to have treated these men in the resolute and uncompromising manner that he did. To use a common expression, he would have been under their thumb and would have had to conciliate them and retain their silence by concessions, by flattery and by trimming his course to their requirements. This the Prophet never did; he was as independent of them as of any other men. He rebuked unrighteousness in them as strongly as he did in others; and when their conduct could no longer be tolerated in the Church of God, he and the Saints withdrew fellowship from them. This is not the way of an impostor, but of an honest, fearless man, who knows his cause is just and puts his trust in God. Neither did any one of the eight witnesses ever turn from his testimony and deny its truthfulness. They ever maintained that their statement was the truth and nothing but the truth. They have all gone beyond the vail now, to receive their reward; and all but one died faithful members of the Church of Jesus Christ of Latter-day Saints.

In considering the nature and value of the testimony of the Prophet Joseph and the three witnesses, the following remarks by Elder Orson Pratt are most pertinent: "No reasonable person will say that these four persons were themselves deceived; the nature of their testimony is such that they must either be bold, daring impostors, or else the Book of Mormon is true. They testify that they saw the angel descend, they heard his voice, they saw the plates in his hand, they saw the engravings upon them as the angel turned them over leaf after leaf, at the same time they heard the voice of the Lord out of the heavens. What greater evidence could they have? They could have had nothing that would have given them greater assurance. If they were deceived there is no certainty in anything. If these four men could be deceived in seeing an angel descend from heaven, on the same grounds the apostles may have been deceived in seeing the Savior ascend up to heaven.''

Then in answer to the suggestion that it is probable that these four men had conspired together to deceive mankind, Brother Pratt asks:

"Is it probable that four men who were, for the most of their days, strangers to each other, residing in three or four different counties, should combine together to testify that they had seen an angel and heard his voice, and also the voice of God, bearing testimony to the truth of the Book of Mormon, when no such thing had happened? Three of these witnesses, namely, Joseph Smith, Oliver Cowdery and David Whitmer, were young men from twenty to twenty-five years of age; they were men who had been accustomed from their childhood to the peaceful vocations of a farmer's life.   Unacquainted with the deceptions, which are more or less practiced in large towns and cities, they possessed the open honesty and simplicity so generally characteristic of country people.   Is it, in the least degree, probable that men so young and inexperienced, accustomed to a country life, and unacquainted with the world at large, would be so utterly abandoned to every thing that was good, so perfectly reckless as to their own future welfare, so heaven-daring and blasphemous as to testify to all nations that which, if false, would forever seal their damnation?   *   *   *   We are not aware that there ever were three, or four, or five impostors who originated an imposition, and succeeded in palming it upon the world as a message from God.   Such a thing might barely be possible, but such a thing would be highly improbable.'' *

---

* ——From "Divine Authenticity of the Book of Mormon "

CHAPTER XI.

OLIVER COWDERY.

OLIVER COWDERY is the first of the three witnesses. He was severed from the Church for immoral conduct during the time that the Saints were in Missouri. Often after his separation from the Church efforts were made to prevail upon him to deny his testimony, but always without effect. At all times, in all places, before all people he continually bore record when the subject of the Book of Mormon was introduced, "Gentlemen, I saw an angel, and I know who that angel was." No amount of cross-questioning could weaken his testimony or confuse his statements on this point. We now copy, from the *Deseret News*, a very interesting episode that occurred during the last few months of his life:

"At a special conference at Council Bluffs, Iowa, held on the 21st of October, in the year 1848, Brother Oliver Cowdery, one of the three important witnesses to the truth of the Book of Mormon, and who had been absent from the Church, through disaffection, for a number of years, and had been engaged in the practice of law, was present and made the remarks here annexed. Brother Orson Hyde presided at the said conference. Brother Reuben Miller, now Bishop of Mill Creek Ward [since deceased] was also present at the time and noted what he said, and has furnished us, what he believes to be a verbatim report of his remarks, which we take pleasure in laying before our readers:

"'Friends and brethren, my name is Cowdery—Oliver Cowdery. In the early history of this Church I stood identified with her, and one in her councils. True it is that the gifts and callings of God are without repentance. Not because I was better than the rest of mankind was I called; but, to fulfill the purposes of God, He called me to a high and holy calling. I wrote, with my own pen, the entire Book of Mormon (save a few pages), as it fell from the lips of the Prophet Joseph Smith, as he translated it by the gift and power of God, by the means of the Urim and Thummim, or, as it is called by that book, 'holy interpreters.' *I beheld with my eyes and handled with my hands the gold plates from which it was translated.* I also saw with my eyes and handled with my hands the 'holy interpreters.' That book is *true.* Sidney Rigdon did not write it. Mr. Spaulding did not write it. I wrote it myself as it fell from the lips of the Prophet. It contains the everlasting gospel, and came forth to the children of men in fulfillment of the revelation of John, where he says he saw an angel come with the everlasting gospel to preach to every nation, kindred, and people. It contains principles of salvation; and if you, my hearers, will walk by its light and obey its precepts, you will be saved with an everlasting salvation in the kingdom of God on high. Brother Hyde has just said that it is very important that we keep and walk in the true channel, in order to avoid sand-bars. This is true. The channel is here. The holy Priesthood is here. I was present with Joseph when an holy angel from God came down from heaven and conferred on us or restored the lesser or Aaronic Priesthood, and said to us, at the same time, that it should remain upon the earth while the earth stands. I was also present with Joseph when the higher or Melchisedek Priesthood was conferred by the holy angel from on high. This Priesthood was then conferred on each other, by the will and commandment of God. This Priesthood, as was then declared, is also to remain upon the earth until the last remnant of time. This holy Priesthood or authority we then conferred upon many, and is just as good and valid as though God had done it in person. I laid my hands upon that man —yes, I laid my right hand upon his head (pointing to Brother Hyde), and I conferred upon him this Priesthood, and he holds that Priesthood now. He was also called through me, by the prayer of faith, an Apostle of the Lord Jesus Christ.' "

CHAPTER XII.

DAVID WHITMER.

DAVID WHITMER, the second of the three witnesses, still lives. His home is in Richmond, Ray Co., Missouri. He left the Church during the dark days of persecution in Missouri and has never returned to the communion of the Saints. He even to this day holds some very bitter feelings toward the Prophet Joseph, whom he wrongfully imagines endeavored to injure him. But notwithstanding these feelings and the fact that he is not a member of the Church he has all the days of his life testified to the divine origin of the Book of Mormon. His word in this respect has never wavered.

Of late various testimonies given to visitors or written by David Whitmer have been widely published in the public newspapers. We subjoin extracts from one or two of these. The first is a portion of a statement signed by himself and dated at Richmond, March 19th, 1881:

"*Unto all Nations, Kindreds, Tongues and People, unto whom these presents shall come:*

"It having been represented by one John Murphy, of Polo, Caldwell county, Missouri, that I, in a conversation with him last Summer, denied my testimony as one of the three witnesses to the 'Book of Mormon:'

"To the end, therefore, that he may understand me now, if he did not then; and that the world may know the truth, I wish now, standing as it were, in the very sunset of life, and in the fear of God, once for all to make this public statement:

"That I have never at any time, denied that testimony or any part thereof, which has so long since been published with that book, as one of the three witnesses. Those who know me best well know that I have always adhered to that testimony. And that no man may be misled or doubt my present views in regard to the same, I do again affirm the truth of all my statements as then made and published.

"'He that hath an ear to hear, let him hear;' it was no delusion; what is written, is written, and he that readeth, let him understand.''

The following are portions of a letter to the Chicago *Times*, detailing the visit of one of its correspondents to Mr. Whitmer, on October 14th, 1881. The statements are given [as those of David Whitmer, and though exceedingly correct as a whole, sometimes, owing to the correspondent's want of familiarity with the subject, they make the speaker fall into slight blunders on historical and other points. He writes:

"The plates from which the book was translated, supposed to be gold, were found in the latter part of the year 1827 or 1828, prior to the acquaintance on Mr. Whitmer's part, with Joseph Smith, and he was loth to believe in their actuality, notwithstanding the community in which he lived (Ontario county, New York), was alive with excitement in regard to Smith's finding a great treasure, and they informed him that they knew that Smith had the plates, as they had seen the place that he had taken them from, on the hill Cumorah, about two miles from Palmyra, N. Y. It was not until June, 1828, that he met the future Prophet, who visited at his father's house, and while there completed the translation of the Book of Mormon, and thus he became conversant with its history, having witnessed Smith dictate to Oliver Cowdery the translation of the characters that were inscribed on the plates, said by Mr. Anthon, our Egyptian scholar, to resemble the characters of that ancient people. Christian Whitmer, his brother, occasionally assisted Cowdery in writing, as did Mrs. Joseph Smith, who was a Miss Hale before she was married.

"In regard to finding the plates, he was told by Smith that they were in a stone casket, and the place where it was deposited, in the hill Cumorah, was pointed out to him by a celestial personage, clad in a dazzling white robe, and he was informed by it that it was the history of the Nephites, a nation that had passed away, whose founders belonged to the days of the tower of Babel. The plates which Mr. Whitmer saw were in the shape of a tablet, fastened with three rings, about one-third of which appeared to be loose, in plates, the other solid, but with perceptible marks where the plates seemed to be sealed, and the guide that pointed it out to Smith very impressively reminded him that the loose plates alone were to be used, the sealed portion was not to be tampered with.

"After the plates had been translated, which process required about six months, the same heavenly visitant appeared and reclaimed the gold tablets of the ancient people informing Smith that he would replace them with other records of the lost tribes that had been brought with them during their wanderings from Asia, which would be forthcoming when the world was ready to receive them. At that time Mr. Whitmer saw the tablets, gazed with awe on the celestial messenger, heard him speak and say: "Blessed is the Lord and he that keeps His commandments;" and then, as he held the plates and turned them over with his hands, so that they could be plainly visible, a voice that seemed to fill all space, musical as the sighing of a wind through the forest, was heard, saying: "What you see is true; testify to the same." And Oliver Cowdery and David Whitmer, standing there, felt, as the white garments of the angel faded from their vision and the heavenly voice still rang in their ears, that it was no delusion—that it was a fact, and they so recorded it. In a day or two after, the same spirit appeared to Martin Harris while he was in company with Smith, and told him also to bear witness to its truth, which he did, as can be seen in the book. Harris described the visitant to Whitmer, who recognized it as the same that he and Cowdery had seen.

"The tablets or plates were translated by Smith, who used a small oval or kidney-shaped stone, called Urim and Thummim, that seemed endowed with the marvelous power of converting the characters on the plates, when used by Smith, into English, who would then dictate to Cowdery what to write. Frequently one character would make two lines of manuscript while others made but a word or two words. Mr. Whitmer emphatically asserts, as did Harris and Cowdery, that while Smith was dictating the translation he had *no manuscript notes or other means of knowledge*, save the Seer stone and the characters as shown on the plates, he being present and cognizant how it was done.

"In regard to the statement that Sidney Rigdon had purloined the work of one Spaulding, a Presbyterian preacher, who had written a romance entitled the 'Manuscript Found,' Mr. Whitmer says there is no foundation for such an assertion. The 'Book of Mormon' was translated in the Summer of 1829, and printed that Winter at Palmyra, New York, and was in circulation before Sidney Rigdon knew anything concerning the Church of Christ, as it was known then. His attention was specially brought to it by the appearance at his church, near Kirtland, Ohio, in the Fall of 1830, of Parley Pratt and Oliver Cowdery, he being at that time a Reformed or Christian preacher, they having been sent west by the Church in New York during that Summer as evangelists, and they carried with them the printed book, the first time that he knew such a thing was in existence.

*   *   *   *   *   *   *

Mr. Whitmer emphatically asserts that he has heard Rigdon, in the pulpit, and in private conversation, declare that the 'Spaulding story,' that he had used a book called the 'Manuscript Found' for the purpose of preparing the 'Book of Mormon,' was as false as were many other charges that were then being made against the infant Church, and he assures me that the story is as untruthful as it is ridiculous.

"In his youth Joseph Smith was quite illiterate, knew nothing of grammar or composition, but obtained quite a good education after he came west; was a man of great magnetism, made friends easily, was liberal and noble in his impulses, tall, finely-formed and full of animal life, but sprang from the most humble circumstances. The first good suit of clothes he had ever worn was presented to him by Christian Whitmer, brother of David.

*   *   *   *   *   *

"Mr. Whitmer's beliefs have undergone no change since his early manhood; he has refused to affiliate with any of the various branches that have sprung up through false teachings, and rests his hopes of the future 'in the teachings of Christ, the apostles and the prophets, and the morals and principles enunciated in the scriptures; that the Book of Mormon is but the testimony of another nation concerning the truth and divinity of Christ and the Bible, and that is his rock, his gospel and his salvation.' Seeing, with him, is believing. He is now as firm in the faith of the divinity of the book that he saw translated as he was when the glory of the celestial visitant almost blinded him with the gleam of his glowing presence, fresh from the Godhead; and the voice, majestic, ringing out from the earth to the mighty dome of space, still lingers in his ears like a chime of silver bells."

The *Deseret Evening News* at the time of the publication of his letter corrected some of the errors of this correspondent. We cannot do better than use its language :

"The first [error] is that the founders of the Nephites 'belonged to the tower of Babel.' The Nephites sprang from Nephi, the son of Lehi, who came to this land from Judea, in the reign of King Zedekiah. The Jaredites, whose history is briefly given in the Book of Mormon, were a distinct and preceding race; they descended from a colony that peopled this country after the dispersion from Babel. The term 'lost tribes' is also incorrect, as the Nephites had no identity with the lost tribes of Israel, being descendants of Joseph, the son of Jacob.

"The next mistake is that 'In a day or two after David Whitmer and Oliver Cowdery saw the angel and the plates, the same spirit appeared to Martin Harris.' The truth is that it was shortly after, on the same day. Martin Harris was with Joseph, Oliver and David, but there was no answer to their prayers, until Martin, who felt that his lack of faith was a hindrance, withdrew. Then the angel appeared, and after the vision closed, Joseph Smith went to the place where Martin Harris was, a little distance off, and joined with him in prayer, when the angel again appeared, and Martin rejoicingly bore testimony that he had seen and heard as the others.

"The next error is that the seer stone which Joseph used in the translation 'was called Urim and Thummim.' The instrument thus denominated was composed of two crystal stones 'set in the two rims of a bow.' The seer stone was separate and distinct from the Urim and Thummim. The latter was delivered to the angel as well as the plates after the translation was completed; the former remained with the Church and is now in the possession of the President."

A still later interviewer gives the following as David Whitmer's testimony to the party of visitors of which the writer was one:

"We asked him if his testimony was the same now as it was at the time the Book of Mormon was published regarding seeing the plates and the angel. He rose to his feet, stretched out his hands and said: 'These hands handled the plates, these eyes saw the angel, and these ears heard His voice; and I know it was of God.'"

Our concluding extract is a statement made by David Whitmer to Elders Orson Pratt and Joseph F. Smith, when these brethren visited him at his home in September, 1878.

In answer to Elder Pratt's question, if he remembered the date he saw the plates, he answered:

"It was in June, 1829—the latter part of the month, and the eight witnesses saw them, I think, the next day or the day after. Joseph showed them the plates himself, but the angel showed us [the three witnesses] the plates, as I suppose to fulfill the words of the book itself. Martin Harris was not with us at this time; he obtained a view of them afterwards [the same day]. Joseph, Oliver, and myself were together when I saw them. We not only saw the plates of the Book of Mormon but also the brass plates, the plates of the Book of Ether, the plates containing the records of the wickedness and secret combinations of the people of the world down to the time of their being engraved and many other plates. The fact is, it was just as though Joseph, Oliver and I were sitting just here on a log when we were overshadowed by a light. It was not like the light of the sun nor like that of a fire, but more glorious and beautiful. It extended away around us, I cannot tell how

far, but in the midst of this light about as far off as he sits
(pointing to John C. Whitmer, sitting a few feet from him),
there appeared, as it were, a table with many records or plates
upon it besides the plates of the Book of Mormon; also the
sword of Laban, the directors—*i. e.* the ball which Lehi had,
and the Interpreters. I saw them just as plain as I see this
bed (striking the bed beside him with his hand), and I heard
the voice of the Lord as distinctly as I ever heard anything in
my life, declaring that the records of the plates of the Book
of Mormon were translated by the gift and power of God.'

"Elder Pratt then asked, 'Did you see the angel at this
time?'

"David Whitmer answered, 'Yes; he stood before us. Our
testimony as recorded in the Book of Mormon is strictly and
absolutely true, just as it is there written.'"

CHAPTER XIII.

MARTIN HARRIS.

IT is probable that many of our readers have seen Martin
Harris.* It is but a few years since he died in our midst.
Though his name is signed last to the testimony of the three
witnesses he was considerable older than the other two.

Martin Harris was the instrument used by the Lord to enable
Joseph to print the Book of Mormon. He supplied the funds
necessary to pay the printer. All of this was repaid to him,
by Joseph, and as he said, "more too." We mention this
because it has been falsely asserted that Joseph made Martin
Harris his dupe and never paid back the money he borrowed
of him.

Brother Harris was a well-to-do farmer at the time he
became acquainted with the Prophet Joseph. He was
respected and esteemed by his neighbors, but like all the others
who had anything to do with the publication of the Book of

---

*——Brother M. Harris, accompanied by Elder E. Stevenson reached
Ogden on the 29th of August, 1870; he afterwards resided until his death at
the home of his son in Smithfield, Cache county.

Mormon, he was assailed with savage bitterness, and accused of numerous sins as soon as it was known that he was a believer in that holy book. He was charged with being visionary, cruel and untruthful, and with having beaten his wife and turned her out of doors.

We will now refer to the testimony of the Kelley brothers, which we quoted when we considered the character of Joseph the Prophet. We found they asked the old residents of Manchester some questions with regard to the reputation of Martin Harris. Those who knew him, invariably spoke well of him. One said, "He was an honorable farmer; he was not very religious before the Book of Mormon was published." Another stated "Harris was an industrious, honest man." A third affirmed "He was an honorable man. He was one of the first men of the town." And so on, one after another denied the calumnies that had been heaped upon the head of this inoffensive, though somewhat peculiar gentleman, whose worst act in the eyes of these neighbors was that he helped Joseph Smith to give the Book of Mormon to the world.

It will be remembered that the testimony of the three witnesses, with regard to the plates from which the Book of Mormon was translated, is to the effect that "We also know that they have been translated by the gift and power of God, for His voice hath declared it unto us; wherefore we know of a surety that the work is true. And we also testify that we have seen the engravings which are upon the plates; and they have been shown unto us by the power of God and not of man. And we declare with words of soberness, that an angel of God came down from heaven, and He brought and laid before our eyes, that we beheld and saw the plates and the engravings thereon." But it must be remembered that this was not the only time that Martin Harris saw the plates. He states that on one occasion he held them on his knee for an hour and a half, and also affirms that "as many of the plates as Joseph Smith translated I handled with my hands, plate after plate." This testimony was given when Harris was not a member of the Church.

Early in the history of the Latter-day Saints Martin Harris became disaffected. He committed grave errors and gave way to a very unchristian-like spirit. The communion of the Saints was withdrawn from him and he became an outcast to the blessings of the gospel. Thus he remained many years, or more than a third of a century, but in his old age he returned as a wandering sheep to the true fold, and again became a partaker of the gifts and blessings of the everlasting gospel. We will now insert an interview had with him when he was not a member of the Church (in 1853?) and two letters written by him nearly twenty years afterwards, after he had renewed his covenant with the Lord at the waters of baptism.

September 15th, 1853.

"Be it known to all whom this may concern that I, David B. Dille, of Ogden City, Weber county, Salt Lake, *en route* to Great Britain, having business with one Martin Harris, formerly of the Church of Latter-day Saints, and residing at Kirtland, Lake county, Ohio, did personally wait upon him at his residence, and found him sick in bed; and was informed by the said Martin Harris that he had not been able to take any nourishment for the space of three days. This, together with his advanced age, had completely prostrated him. After making my business known to Mr. Harris, and some little conversation with him, the said Martin Harris started up in bed, and, after particularly inquiring concerning the prosperity of the Church, made the following declaration:

'I feel that a spirit has come across me—the old spirit of Mormonism; and I begin to feel as I used to feel; and I will not say—'I won't go to the valley.' Then addressing himself to his wife, he said—'I don't know but that, if you will get me some breakfast, I will get up and eat it.'

"I then addressed Mr. Harris relative to his once high and exalted station in the Church, and his then fallen and afflicted condition. I afterwards put the following questions to Mr. Harris, to which he severally replied with the greatest cheerfulness: 'What do you think of the Book of Mormon? Is it a divine record?'

"Mr. Harris replied: 'I was the right hand man of Joseph Smith, and I know that he was a prophet of God. I know the Book of Mormon is true—*and you know that I know that it is true.* I know that the plates have been translated by the gift and power of God, for His voice declared it unto us; therefore I know of a surety that the work is true; *for did I not at one time hold the plates on my knee an hour and a half,* while in conversation with Joseph, when we went to bury them in the woods, that the enemy might not obtain them? Yes, I did. *And as many of the plates as Joseph Smith translated,*

I handled with my hands, plate after plate.' Then, describing their dimensions, he pointed with one of the fingers of his left hand to the back of his right hand and said: 'I should think they were so long,' or about eight inches, 'and about so thick,' or about four inches; 'and each of the plates was thicker than the thickest tin.'

"I then asked Mr. Harris if he ever lost 3,000 dollars by the publishing of the Book of Mormon?

"Mr Harris said, 'I never lost one cent. Mr. Smith paid me all that I advanced, and more too.' As much as to say he received a portion of the profits accruing from the sale of the books.

"Mr. Harris further said: 'I took a transcript of the characters of the plates to Dr. Anthon, of New York. When I arrived at the house of Professor Anthon, I found him in his office and alone, and presented the transcript to him, and asked him to read it. He said if I would bring the plates, he would assist in the translation. I told him I could not, for they were sealed. Professor Anthon then gave me a certificate certifying that the characters were Arabic, Chaldaic and Egyptian. I then left Dr. Anthon, and was near the door, when he said, 'How did the young man know the plates were there?' I said an angel had shown them to him. Professor Anthon then said, 'Let me see the certificate!' Upon which, I took it from my waistcoat pocket and unsuspectingly gave it to him. He then tore it up in anger, saying, there was no such things as angels now, it was all a hoax. I then went to Dr. Mitchell with the transcript, and he confirmed what Professor Anthon had said.'

"Mr. Harris is about fifty-eight years old, and is on a valuable farm of ninety acres, beautifully situated at Kirtland, Lake county, Ohio."—*Millennial Star.*

"SMITHFIELD, UTAH,
"Nov. 23, 1870.

"*Mr. Emerson,*
     SIR:—I received your favor. In reply I will say concerning the plates, I do say that the angel did show to me the plates containing the Book of Mormon. Further, the translation that I carried to Professor Anthon was copied from these same plates; also, that the professor did testify to it being a correct translation. I do firmly believe and do know that Joseph Smith was a prophet of God; for without, I know he could not had that gift; neither could he have translated the same. I can give, if you require it, one hundred witnesses to the proof of the Book of Mormon. I defy any man to show me any passage of scripture that I am not posted on or familiar with. I will answer any question you feel like asking

to the best of my knowledge, if you can rely on my testimony of the same. In conclusion, I can say that I arrived in Utah safe, in good health and spirits, considering the long journey. I am quite well at present, and have been, generally speaking, since I arrived.   With many respects,

"I remain your humble friend,

"MARTIN HARRIS."

"SMITHFIELD, CACHE CO., UTAH.

"January, 1871.

"*To H. Emerson,*

DEAR SIR:—Your second letter, dated December, 1870, came duly to hand.   I am truly glad to see a spirit of inquiry manifested therein.   I reply by a borrowed hand, as my sight has failed me too much to write myself.   Your questions:

"Question 1.   'Did you go to England to lecture against Mormonism?'

"Answer.   I answer emphatically, No, I did not.   No man ever heard me in any way deny the truth of the Book of Mormon, the administration of the angel that showed me the plates; nor the organization of the Church of Jesus Christ of Latter-day Saints, under the administration of Joseph Smith, Jun., the prophet whom the Lord raised up for that purpose in these latter days, that He may show forth His power and glory.   The Lord has shown me these things by His Spirit, by the administration of holy angels, and confirmed the same with signs following, step by step, as the work has progressed, for the space of fifty-three years.

The Lord showed me there was no true church upon the face of the earth, none built upon the foundation designed by the Savior, the rock of revelation, as declared to Peter.   (*See Matt., xvi.*, 16-18.)   He also showed me that an angel should come and restore the holy Priesthood again to the earth, and commission His servants again with the holy gospel to preach to them that dwell on the earth.   (*See Revelation, xiv.,* 6, 7.) He further showed me that the time was nigh when He would 'set His hand again the second time to restore the kingdom of Israel, when He would gather the outcasts of Israel and the dispersed of Judah from the four corners of the earth,' when He would bring the record of Joseph which was in the hand of Ephraim, and join with the record of Judah, when the two records should become one in the hand of the Lord to accomplish His great work of the last days.   (*See Ezekiel, xxxvi, xxxvii; also Isaiah, xxix.,; also Isaiah, lviii. to the end of the book; also Psalms.*)

"Question 2.   'What became of the plates from which the Book of Mormon was translated?'

"Answer. They were returned to the angel, Moroni, from whom they were received, to be brought forth again in the due time of the Lord; for they contain many things pertaining to the gathering of Israel, which gathering will take place in this generation, and shall be testified of among all nations, according to the old prophets; as the Lord will set His ensign to the people, and gather the outcasts of Israel. (*See Isaiah, xi.*)

"Now, dear sir, examine these scriptures carefully; and should there still be any ambiguity relative to this great work of the last days, write again and we will endeavor to enlighten you on any point relative to this doctrine.

"I am, very respectfully,
"MARTIN HARRIS, SEN."

The following interesting statement is an extract from a letter written to the *Deseret News*, by Elder Edward Stevenson:

"Martin Harris related an instance that occurred during the time that he wrote that portion of the translation of the Book of Mormon, which he was favored to write direct from the mouth of the Prophet Joseph Smith. He said that the Prophet possessed a seer stone, by which he was enabled to translate as well as from the Urim and Thummim, and for convenience he then used the seer stone. Martin explained the translation as follows: By aid of the seer stone, sentences would appear and were read by the prophet and written by Martin, and when finished he would say, 'Written,' and if correctly written, that sentence would disappear and another appear in its place, but if not written correctly it remained until corrected, so that the translation was just as it was engraven on the plates, precisely in the language then used. Martin said, after continued translation they would become weary and would go down to the river and exercise by throwing stones out on the river, etc. While so doing on one occasion, Martin found a stone very much resembling the one used for translating, and on resuming their labor of translation, Martin put in place the stone that he had found. He said that the Prophet remained silent unusually and intently gazing in darkness, no traces of the usual sentences appearing. Much surprised, Joseph exclaimed, 'Martin! What is the matter? All is as dark as Egypt.' Martin's countenance betrayed him, and the prophet asked Martin why he had done so. Martin said, to stop the mouths of fools, who had told him that the Prophet had learned those sentences and was merely repeating them, etc.

Martin said further that the seer stone differed in appearance entirely from the Urim and Thummim that was obtained with the plates, which were two clear stones set in two rims, very much resembled spectacles, only they were larger.   Martin said there were not many pages translated while he wrote ; after which Oliver Cowdery did the writing.

In concluding this portion of our subject we desire to draw attention to the entire agreement between the witnesses as to the manner in which the plates were translated.   If any fraud had been practiced, or there had been a conspiracy to deceive, these witnesses in the lapse of so many years would doubtless have told conflicting stories, especially in regard to minor details.   But as it is their statements are harmonious one with the other, their testimony unchangeable and the whole consistent with the narrative of the Prophet Joseph and the condition of things by which they were then surrounded.

CHAPTER XIV.

INTERNAL EVIDENCES OF THE BOOK OF MORMON.

WE will now consider for a short time a few of the internal evidences of the genuineness of the Book of Mormon, or the proofs in itself that it is what it claims to be, a record of God's dealings with the former inhabitants of this continent.

Among the more prominent internal evidences of its genuineness may be mentioned:

1st.   Its historical consistency.

2nd.   The entire absence of all anachronisms, or confusion in its chronology, and of conflicting statements with regard to history, doctrine or prophecy.

3rd.   The purity of its doctrines, and their entire harmony with the teachings of our Savior and His inspired servants as recorded in the Bible.

4th.   Its already fulfilled prophecies.

5th.   Its harmony with the traditions of the Indian races.

6th. Its entire accord with scientific truth; none of its geographical, astronomical or other statements being contrary to what is positively known in these sciences.

There is nothing in the entire historical narrative of the Book of Mormon that is inconsistent with the dealings of the Almighty with mankind, or conflicting with history as far as the history which has been handed down to us in other records deals with events referred to in the Book of Mormon. On the other hand, the whole scheme of human salvation, as developed in the dealings of the Lord with the Jaredites, Nephites and Lamanites, gives us the most exalted ideas of His love for His mortal children and His condescension towards the erring sons and daughters of Adam. Even if the Book of Mormon were not true, it deserves to be so, from the sublimity of the ideas that it conveys with regard to God's providences and His ways and methods of leading, directing and preserving His children. No nobler monument to the glory, the mercy and the long-suffering of our Heavenly Father than this wonderful book was ever presented for the consideration of mankind.

It requires a great deal more credulity to believe it possible that any author, ignorant or learned, be he Joseph Smith, Sidney Rigdon or Solomon Spaulding, could, without the inspiration of the Almighty, bring forth such a work as the Book of Mormon, than to believe that it is a revelation from the Almighty.

Hengstenberg, in his work on the Pentateuch, says:

"It is the unavoidable fate of a spurious historical work of any length to be involved in contradictions." This is obviously true. No thinking person will deny that it would be one of the most difficult of all literary feats to compose a historical work extending over thousands of years and dealing with hundreds of individuals without introducing some blunders as to time, place or circumstance, or permitting egregious contradictions to pass unnoticed. But the Book of Mormon is entirely free from all blunders of such a kind. This alone stamps it as of more than human origin. For more than fifty years, the bigoted and skeptical have been endeavoring to find errors, inconsistencies or impossibilities within its contents.

But in this they have utterly failed. Not one of all their pretended discoveries of errors has stood the test of investigation. It has been found, without exception, that in such cases the objector has either dishonestly garbled the text, put an impossible construction on good, plain English, or presented his own private interpretation of the words of the book instead of the words themselves. The writer of this having perused the Book of Mormon many times, confidently asserts that there is no conflict of dates, no contradiction of details, no discordant doctrine, no historical inconsistency, from the commencement of the first Book of Nephi to the end of Moroni. All is a plain, simple narrative, occasionally somewhat unpolished in its style, and here and there at variance with the strict rules of grammar, but throughout maintaining its unities and harmonies, and bearing upon its face indelible marks of its divine origin.

We now come to the doctrinal portions of the work:

It is readily admitted on all hands that no sectarian preacher like Mr. Spaulding would write doctrines, such as the Book of Mormon contains, these doctrines being at variance with the creed that he professed ; and, indeed, in many respects different to those of every creed then extant upon the face of the earth. The Book of Mormon, be it human or divine, is a new revelation on religious matters to this generation, and its entire accord with the revelations of the Almighty contained in the Bible is a proof so strong of its divinity that none have been able to gainsay it. It is utterly ridiculous to imagine that Joseph Smith, unlettered as he was, could have written a work in such entire harmony with the holy scriptures and entering into many new particulars, as it frequently does, with regard to doctrines only slightly touched upon in the Old or New Testaments: it not only harmonizes with the scriptures, but it explains them, makes clear the meaning of many an obscure passage, and while it never conflicts with, it often develops, truths of the utmost importance to humanity.

How wonderful a miracle!—much greater than the discovery of the records in the hill Cumorah—that an uneducated youth, (and neither friend nor foe claims he was educated), could produce a work pregnant with principles connected with the

most vital interests of the human family, and treating on sub-
jects that concern man's temporal and eternal welfare, which
cannot be refuted by all the learned of the world. Would not
this be much more wonderful, calling for a much greater strain
on our credulity than to believe that God had again spoken
and brought to light this long-hidden treasure? And if it be
inconsistent to believe that neither Joseph Smith nor Solomon
Spaulding was the author of the religious portions of the
Book of Mormon, wherein is it more consistent to ascribe the
authorship to Sidney Rigdon? He was as utterly ignorant of
many of the doctrines and principles made plain in the Book
of Mormon as was Solomon Spaulding or any other uninspired
priest of fifty or more years ago. There was no system of
philosophy, ethics or religion then known to mankind from
which he could have drawn the inspiration to write many of
the doctrinal precepts in the Book of Mormon.

To tide over this difficulty, persons unacquainted with the
contents of the Book of Mormon (which unfortunately the
greater portion of mankind are) have suggested that Solomon
Spaulding wrote the historical portion (an impossibility, as we
have heretofore shown) and that Joseph Smith or somebody
else added the religious portion. To those who have read the
Book of Mormon, this hypothesis is supremely ridiculous.

An objector to the Bible might, with equal consistency,
assert that somebody wrote the historical portion of the Old
and New Testaments, and somebody else, after the historical
portion was all written, introduced the religious teachings.
One is as impossible as the other. Every one who knows
anything of the Book of Mormon knows that the narrative
of events grows out of and is inseparably connected with the
religious idea. The book opens with the statement that Lehi
was a prophet, bearing Jehovah's unwelcome message of
destruction to the inhabitants of the sin-seared city of Jerusalem. They rejected and persecuted him. By divine com-
mand he fled with his family into the wilderness and was led
by that same inspiratian to the American continent. The reason
why the Lord thus delivered him was, that he might raise up
to Himself a people that would serve Him. He covenanted
to give Lehi and his posterity this most precious land as their

inheritance if they kept His commandments. How they fulfilled His law, how they prospered when obedient, how they
suffered when disobedient, is the burden of the story of the
writers of the Book of Mormon. It is the main idea to which
all others are incidental, the controlling thought around which
all others concentrate; it is the life of the whole record, the
golden thread running through all its pages, which gives consistency to all its parts. A man might just as well attempt to
write the gospel of St. Matthew and leave out all references to
the Lord Jesus Christ, as write the Book of Mormon without
its religious theory and teachings.

The creature who invented the idea of the dual authorship
of this book must have imagined that the doctrinal portion
was dropped in by lumps or clumsily inserted between different
historical epochs. It is true there are places where liberal
extracts from the Bible are quoted, and if these were all, there
might be some semblance of consistency in the supposition.
But it is not so, the doctrinal and historical portions are, as a
general thing, so intermingled and blended that neither could
be withdrawn without destroying the sense of the other. If it
were possible to conceive of the amalgamation of two separate
documents—one religious and the other historical—it would be
much easier to believe that the doctrinal portions were written
first and that the historical ideas were afterwards filled in; for,
as before mentioned, the historical narrative is but secondary
and tributary to the religious idea. But this would not sup-
port the theory of the Spauldingites; it would, in fact, entirely
upset all their arguments for the reason that they claim that
the "Manuscript Found," a historical romance of an idolatrous
people, be it remembered, was written by Spaulding not later
than 1812, while the Book of Mormon was not published by
Joseph Smith until 1830, consequently such an arrangement
would be fatal to their hypothesis.

We next glance at the prophecies of the Book of Mormon,
a number of which are already fulfilled. These are among the
most irrefutable evidences of the divinity of the work; the
facts are patent to all the world, they are within the reach of
all mankind. Ever since the year 1830, men have had the
opportunity of testing the contents of the Book of Mormon,

as it has not been hidden in a corner, but has been published in all the dominant languages of Christendom. To say that many of its prophecies have not been fulfilled is to deny history. And it cannot be asserted that these prophecies are happy guesses, as, at the time when the Book of Mormon was published, they appeared most improbable, none more so than those which foretell the results that would follow its own publication. For it must be remembered that when it was published there was no Church of Jesus Christ organized upon the earth, and there was no remote probability of the then non-existent church producing the results in itself and to the world that the Book of Mormon declares should follow its establishment, which have been fulfilled, year by year, from the time of its publication to the present. If the Book of Mormon be not true, then these prophecies originated with Joseph Smith, and, as they have been fulfilled, he was a true prophet; further, as they were declared in the name of the Lord and the Lord has recognized them by permitting their fulfillment in so many wondrous ways and by such direct manifestations of His divine power, therefore the conclusion is inevitable that the Lord owned and acknowledged Joseph Smith as His servant. On the other hand, if they did not originate with Joseph Smith, then the record is genuine, for the prophecies are true, and they were uttered by the men to whom they are ascribed. If so, Joseph's account of his discovery of the plates is true and he was a seer and a revelator, especially called of God to lay the foundation of the mighty work of the last days.

Those who are so strongly opposed to "Mormonism" can accept whichever horn of the dilemma they choose. But to our mind the first supposition is utterly untenable, as it is impossible for us to conceive that God, who hateth a lie, would choose for His servant a man who made such a science of falsehood; or that the Divine One would add the seal of His approbation to a forgery and an imposture, such as the Book of Mormon would be under these circumstances. To believe such a thing, would be as consistent as to believe that if there were prophecies contained in "Gulliver's Travels" the Lord would move heaven and earth to bring about their fulfillment; for if the Book of Mormon be not what it claims, then it is as

4*

much a romance as the celebrated work of Dean Swift, and one is as worthy of credence as the other.

CHAPTER XV.
THE PROPHECIES OF THE BOOK OF MORMON.

LET us now consider a few of the fulfilled prophecies of the Book of Mormon. On page 581 it is stated: "And behold ye [the translator] may be privileged that ye may shew the plates unto those who shall assist to bring forth this work; and *unto three shall they be shewn by the power of God;* wherefore they shall know of a surety that these things are true. And in the mouth of three witnesses shall these things be established; and the testimony of three and this work   *   * shall stand as a testimony against the world at the last day" (*Ether v. 2-4.*)

In the above we have the statement that three witnesses are to be raised up by the power of God to testify to the truth and genuineness of the book. At the commencement of the Book of Mormon we have the testimony of these three witnesses— Oliver Cowdery, David Whitmer and Martin Harris—to the fulfillment of the above prophecy. They declare that an angel of God came down from heaven, who brought the plates and laid them before their eyes. "Ah, but," says our opponent, "what an easy matter it would be for an impostor like Joseph Smith to conspire with three other men to fulfill the prophecy?" Such a thing is quite supposable to ignorant persons unacquainted with the matter, but very improbable under the circumstances as already shown. Or Joseph Smith might even have deceived three men had he shown them the plates himself; but not all the impostors in the world could bring an angel down from heaven, or cause the Lord to declare with His own voice that the plates were translated by His gift and power. In this is the utter impossibility. As we have before shown these three men under all circumstances have borne one continuous, undeviating testimony that they saw the angel and heard the voice, and that their testimony in the Book of Mormon is true. No amount of sophistry can persuade the sincere investigator into these matters that Joseph Smith had sufficient cunning and dexterity, even if he had appliances, to deceive these three men into the belief that they had actually seen an angel descend from heaven and present them the plates for their examination. This is altogether too great a stretch for the imagination of an ordinarily sane person.

It is more difficult to select isolated passages from the prophecies of the Book of Mormon than from those of the Bible; for as a general thing they are so intimately associated with the context that their force, power and meaning are surprisingly weakened when quoted alone. Among the prophecies of Mormon's record that are partially fulfilled or are now in process of fulfillment may be mentioned those relating to—

The carrying of the Book itself to the Indians, and their acceptance of its truths.

The beginning of the gathering of the Jews to their ancient home in Canaan.

The establishment of Christ's Church, and the spilling of the blood of the Saints by the wicked.

The great increase of corruption among those who reject the gospel message.

The formation of numerous powerful secret societies for the purpose of murder, plunder and gain, and for the overthrowal of governments and nations.

We append a few of these prophecies:

"And now behold, I say unto you, that when the Lord shall see fit, in His wisdom, that these sayings shall come forth unto the Gentiles, according to His word then ye may know that the covenant which the Father hath made with the children of Israel, concerning their restoration to the lands of their inheritance, is already beginning to be fulfilled" (*III. Nephi xxix.* 1).

"And then shall the work of the Father commence at that day, even when this gospel shall be preached among the remnant of this people [the Indians]. Verily I say unto you, at that day shall the work of the Father commence among all the dispersed of my people; yea, even the tribes which have been lost, which the Father hath led away out of Jerusalem. Yea, the work shall commence among all the dispersed of my people, with the Father, to prepare the way whereby they may come unto me, that they may call on the Father in my name. Yea, and then shall the work commence, with the Father among all nations, in preparing the way whereby His people may be gathered home to the land of their inheritance. And they shall go out from all nations; and they shall not go out in haste, nor go by flight, for I will go before them, saith the Father, and I will be their rearward'' (*III. Nephi xxi.* 26-29).

"And there are also secret combinations, even as in times of old, according to the combinations of the devil, for he is the foundation of all these things; yea, the foundation of murder, and works of darkness, yea, and he leadeth them by the neck with a flaxen cord, until he bindeth them with his strong cords for ever" (*II. Nephi xxvi.* 22).

"And whatsoever nation shall uphold such secret combinations, to get power and gain, until they shall spread over the nation, behold, they shall be destroyed, for the Lord will not suffer that the blood of His Saints, which shall be shed by them, shall always cry unto Him from the ground for vengeance upon them, and yet He avenge them not;

"Wherefore, O ye Gentiles, it is wisdom in God that these things should be shewn unto you, that thereby ye may repent of your sins, and suffer not that these murderous combinations shall get above you, which are built up to get power and gain, and the work, yea, even the work of destruction come upon you, yea, even the sword of the justice of the eternal God shall fall upon you, to your overthrow and destruction, if ye shall suffer these things to be;

"Wherefore the Lord commandeth you, wh n ye shall see these things come among you, that ye shall awake to a sense of your awful situation, because of this secret combination which shall be among you, or wo be unto it, because of the blood of them who have been slain; for they cry from the dust for vengeance upon it, and also upon those who built it up.

"For it cometh to pass that whoso buildeth it up, seeketh to overthrow the freedom of all lands, nations, and countries; and it bringeth to pass the destruction of all people, for it is built up by the devil, who is the father of all lies; even that same liar who beguiled our first parents; yea, even that same liar who hath caused man to commit murder from the beginning; who hath hardened the hearts of men, that they have murdered the prophets, and stoned them, and cast them out from the beginning" (*Ether viii.* 22-25).

"And no one need say, They shall not come, for they surely shall, for the Lord hath spoken it; for out of the earth shall they come, by the hand of the Lord, and none can stay it; and it shall come in a day when it shall be said that miracles are done away; and it shall come even as if one should speak from the dead.

"And it shall come in a day when the blood of the Saints shall cry unto the Lord, because of secret combinations and the works of darkness;

"Yea, it shall come in a day when the power of God shall be denied, and churches become defiled, and shall be lifted up in the pride of their hearts; yea, even in a day when leaders of churches, and teachers, in the pride of their hearts, even to the envying of them who belong to their churches" (*Mormon viii* 26-28).

"Yea, why do you build up your secret abominations to get gain, and cause that widows should mourn before the Lord, and also orphans to mourn before the Lord; and also the blood of their fathers and their husbands to cry unto the Lord from the ground, for vengeance upon your heads?

"Behold, the sword of vengeance hangeth over you; and the time soon cometh that He avengeth the blood of the Saints upon you, for He will not suffer their cries any longer" (*Mormon viii.* 40-1).

For further information on this subject we refer our readers to President George Q. Cannon's admirable "Life of Nephi," wherein the prophecies of that ancient worthy are considered in much detail, and with great care and plainness.

In conclusion to sum up the internal evidence, we will adopt the words of Elder Orson Pratt:

"If the historical parts of the Book of Mormon be compared with what little is known from other sources concerning the history of ancient America, there will be found much evidence to substantiate its truth; but there cannot be found one truth among all the gleanings of antiquity that clashes with the historical truth of the Book of Mormon.

"If the prophetical part of this wonderful book be compared with the prophetical declarations of the Bible, there will be found much evidence in the latter to establish the truth of the former. But though there are many predictions in the Book of Mormon, relating to the great events of the last days, which the Bible gives us no information about, yet there is nothing in the predictions of the Bible that contradict in the least, the predictions in the Book of Mormon

"If the doctrinal part of the Book of Mormon be compared with the doctrines of the Bible, there will be found the same perfect harmony which we find on the comparison of the prophetical parts of the two books. Although there are many points of the doctrine of Christ that are far more plain and definite in the Book of Mormon than in the Bible, and many things revealed in relation to doctrine that never could be fully learned from the Bible, yet there are not any items of doctrine in the two sacred books that contradict each other or clash in the least.

"If the various books which enter into the collection, called the Book of Mormon, be carefully compared with each other, there will be found nothing contradicting in history, in prophecy, or in doctrine.

"If the miracles of the Book of Mormon be compared with the miracles of the Bible, there cannot be found in the former any thing that would be more difficult to believe, than what we find in the latter.

"If we compare the historical, prophetical and doctrinal parts of the Book of Mormon with the great truths of science and nature, we find no contradictions, no absurdities, nothing unreasonable. The most perfect harmony therefore exists between the great truths revealed in the Book of Mormon and all known truths, whether religious, historial, or scientific."

APPENDIX.

MRS. MATILDA SPAULDING MCKINSTRY'S STATEMENT REGARDING THE "MANU-
SCRIPT FOUND:"

WASHINGTON, D. C. April 3rd, 1880.

So much has been published that is erroneous concerning the "Manuscript Found," written by my father, the Rev. Solomon Spaulding, and its supposed connection with the book called the Mormon Bible, I have willingly consented to make the following statement regarding it, repeating all that I remember personally of this manuscript, and all that is of importance which my mother related to me in connection with it, at the same time affirming that I am in tolerable health and vigor, and that my memory, in common with elderly people, is clearer in regard to the events of my earlier years, rather than those of my maturer life.

During the war of 1812, I was residing with my parents in a little town in Ohio called Conneaut. I was then in my sixth year. My father was in business there, and I remember his iron foundry and the men he had at work, but that he remained at home most of the time, and was reading and writing a great deal. He frequently wrote little stories, which he read to me. There were some round mounds of earth near our house which greatly interested him, and he said a tree on the top of one of them was a thousand years old. He set some of his men to work digging into one of these mounds, and I vividly remember how excited he became when he heard that they had exhumed some human bones, portions of gigantic skeletons, and various relics.

He talked with my mother of these discoveries in the mound, and was writing every day as the work progressed. Afterward he read the manuscript which I had seen him writing, to the neighbors, and to a clergyman, a friend of his who came to see him. Some of the names that he mentioned while reading to these people I have never forgotten. They are as fresh to me to-day as though I heard them yesterday. They were *Mormon, Maroni, Lamenite, Nephi.*

We removed from Conneaut to Pittsburg while I was still very young, but every circumstance of this removal is distinct in my memory. In that city my father had an intimate friend named Patterson, and I frequently visited Mr. Patterson's library with him, and heard my father talk about books with him. In 1816 my father died at Amity, Pennsylvania, and directly after his death my mother and myself went to visit at the residence of my mother's brother, William H. Sabine, at Onondaga Valley, Onondaga county, New York. Mr. Sabine was a lawyer of distinction and wealth, and greatly respected. We carried all our personal effects with us, and one of these was an old trunk, in which my mother had placed all my father's writings which had been preserved. I perfectly remember the appearance of this trunk, and of looking at its contents. There were sermons and other papers, and I saw a manuscript about an inch thick, closely written, tied with some of the stories my father had written for me, one of which he called "The Frogs of Wyndham." On the outside of this manuscript were written the words, "Manuscript Found." I did not read it, but looked through it and had it in my hands many times, and saw the names I had heard at Conneaut, when my father read it to his friends. I was about eleven years of age at this time.

After we had been at my uncle's for some time, my mother left me there and went to her father's house at Pomfret, Connecticut, but did not take her furniture nor the old trunk of manuscript with her. In 1820 she married Mr. Davison, of Hartwicks, a village near Cooperstown, New York, and sent for the things she had left at Onondaga Valley, and I remember that the old trunk, with its contents, reach her in safety. In 1828, I was married to Dr. A. McKinstry, of Hampden county, Massachusetts, and went there to reside. Very soon after my mother joined me there, and was with me most of the time until her death in 1844. We heard, not long after she came to live with me—I do not remember just how long—something of Mormonism, and the report that it had been taken from my father's "Manuscript Found;" and then came to us direct an account of the Mormon meeting at Conneaut, Ohio, and that, on one occasion, when the Mormon Bible was read there in public, my father's brother, John Spaulding, Mr. Lake and many other persons who were present, at once recognized its similarity to the "Manuscript Found," which they had heard read years before by my father in the same town.* There was a great deal of talk and a great deal published at this time about Mormonism all over the country. I believe it was in 1834 that a man named Hurlburt came to my house at Monson to see my mother, who told us that he had been sent by a committee to procure the "Manuscript Found" written by the Rev. Solomon Spaulding, so as to compare it with the Mormon Bible. He

---

* ——A gentleman who resided near Conneaut at that time stated, soon after the first publication of this story regarding Mr. John Spaulding, that he (J. S.) never lived in Conneaut to the writer's most positive knowledge.

presented a letter to my mother from my uncle, Wm. H. Sabine, of Onondaga Valley, in which he requested her to loan this manuscript to Hurlburt, as he (my uncle) was desirous "to uproot" (as he expressed it) "this Mormon fraud." Hurlburt represented that he had been a convert to Mormonism, but had given it up, and through the "Manuscript Found" wished to expose its wickedness. My mother was careful to have me with her in all the conversations she had with Hurlburt, who spent a day at my house. She did not like his appearance, and mistrusted his motives, but having great respect for her brother's wishes and opinions, she reluctantly consented to his request. The old trunk, containing the desired "Manuscript Found," she had placed in the care of Mr. Jerome Clark, of Hartwicks, when she came to Monson, intending to send for it. On the repeated promise of Hurlburt to return the manuscript to us, she gave him a letter to Mr. Clark to open the trunk and deliver it to him. We afterward heard that he had received it from Mr. Clark, at Hartwicks, but from that time we have never had it in our possession, and I have no present knowledge of its existence, Hurlburt never returning it or answering letters requesting him to do so. Two years ago I heard he was still living in Ohio, and with my consent he was asked for the "Manuscript Found." He made no response, although we have evidence that he received the letter containing the request. So far I have stated facts within my knowledge. My mother mentioned many other circumstances to me in connection with this subject which are interesting, of my father's literary tastes, his fine education and peculiar temperament. She stated to me that she had heard the manuscript alluded to read by my father, was familiar with its contents, and she deeply regretted that her husband, as she believed, had innocently been the means of furnishing matter for a religious delusion. She said that my father loaned this "Manuscript Found" to Mr. Patterson, of Pittsburg, and that when he returned it to my father, he said: "Polish it up, finish it, and you will make money out of it." My mother confirmed my remembrances of my father's fondness for history, and told me of his frequent conversations regarding a theory which he had of a prehistoric race which had inhabited this continent, etc., all showing that his mind dwelt on this subject. The "Manuscript Found," she said, was a romance written in Biblical style, and that while she heard it read she had no special admiration for it more than other romances he wrote and read to her. We never, either of us, ever saw, or in any way communicated with the Mormons, save Hurlburt, as above described; and while we have no personal knowledge that the Mormon Bible was taken from the "Manuscript Found," there are many evidences to us that it was and that Hurlburt and others at the time thought so. A convincing proof to us of this belief was that my uncle, William H. Sabine, had undoubtedly read the manuscript while it was in his house, and his faith that its production would show to the world that the Mormon Bible had been taken from it, or was the same with slight alterations. I have frequently answered questions that have been asked by different persons regarding the "Manuscript Found," but until now have never made a statement at length for publication.

    (Signed)   M. S. McKINSTRY.

  Sworn and subscribed to before me this 3rd day of April, A. D. 1880, at the city of Washington, D. C.

                                CHARLES WALTER, Notary Public.

www.ingramcontent.com/pod-product-compliance
Lightning Source LLC
Chambersburg PA
CBHW022344020726
47500CB00004B/1272